RUNNING
WITH THE
WIND

JOHN FOLEY

RUNNING WITH THE WIND

Woodbury, Minnesota

First Edition
First Printing, 2007

Book design by Steffani Sawyer
Cover design by Ellen Dahl
Cover photograph © 2007 DigitalStock
Editing by Rhiannon Ross

Flux, an imprint of Llewellyn Publications

Library of Congress Cataloging-in-Publication Data
Foley, John, 1960–
    Running with the wind / John Foley.—1st ed.
      p. cm.
    Sequel to: Hoops of steel.
    Summary: Struggling to find a direction for his life after his legal guardian dies and his girlfriend goes off to college, high school graduate Jackson O'Connell takes a job working in a boatyard and learns how to sail.
    ISBN 978-0-7387-1002-0
    [1. Boats and boating—Fiction. 2. Sailing—Fiction. 3. Interpersonal relations—Fiction.] I. Title.
    PZ7.F729Ru 2007
    [Fic]—dc22

2007010673

Flux
Llewellyn Publications
A Division of Llewellyn Worldwide, Ltd.
2143 Wooddale Drive, Dept. 978-0-7387-1002-0
Woodbury, MN 55125-2989, U.S.A.
www.fluxnow.com

Printed in the United States of America

For Miss Jules, who lets me go play in the woods and on the water; and for my late father, John Sr., my brother Mike, and my friend Randy Perigen—three fine sailors and finer men.

Also by John Foley

Hoops of Steel
Tundra Teacher

ONE

"Current, in navigation...a certain progressive movement of the water of the sea, by which all bodies floating therein are compelled to alter their course, or velocity, or both, and submit to the laws imposed on them by the current."

—William Falcone

The last time I saw Granny Dwyer alive she was sitting in a lawn chair and knitting a sweater while I did my thing at the regional track meet in Matawan, the last day of May. My thing is the high jump, and I was in top form that day. Granny's chair was on the grass at the edge of the high jump apron, and she clapped and cheered whenever I jumped, but went back to her knitting when my teammates and competitors took their turns.

On my last jump I cleared the bar at six foot seven, a personal best and good enough to win by three inches. That's pretty good hops for a white guy, as my friend Thaddeus Fly put it later. He could probably do seven feet easily if he went out for track, but basketball is his one and only game.

Anyway, Granny waved to me after the meet and said she'd see me at home. I had to shower and change and was getting a ride from Marvin Renker, a shot-putter on the team and a pretty good buddy. He dropped me off and I was walking toward the front door when I heard a thump from inside the house. A small noise, probably nothing. Maybe I didn't even hear a noise, but just sort of sensed it; when I thought about it later, it didn't seem possible that such a little thing could make a sound that I'd hear outside. In any case, I suddenly knew something bad had happened, and I dropped my gym bag and ran inside.

Granny was lying on the floor in the kitchen, legs curled into the fetal position and her left arm flung straight out. When she looked up at me, her eyes looked strangely young again, the way she did in her old pictures. It sounds cold and unfeeling, but I knew she was dying and there was nothing I could do for her. Looking down at her, I just knew. I never tried to explain it to anyone because most people wouldn't understand. They think you have to run around and say "Oh my God!" and make a lot of noise when someone is dying, like on TV. It wasn't like that.

"Jackson," she whispered, and I swear she smiled. I kneeled beside her and softly touched her hair. "You're a good boy. You and Gerry are my good boys. Be happy, Jackson." Then her body seemed to relax and her breath stopped and she was gone.

Right then I should have started CPR. I knew how to do it from a class at school. Kneeling there, I tried to get myself to start three or four times. I checked her vitals—she wasn't breathing and I couldn't find a pulse—and I'd leaned forward to start mouth-to-mouth resuscitation, but just couldn't. I wasn't afraid or freaked out or anything...it just seemed wrong. That's the best I can explain it.

Finally I got up and called 911. "My grandmother collapsed," I told the dispatcher. "I think she died...I think she'd dead." Felt really bad, to say that. I gave the dispatcher the address and she said an ambulance was on the way. I thought some more about trying CPR, then actually said "No!" out loud, like I was having a conversation with myself. Maybe I was freaking out a little, but it was a controlled freak-out.

Even with her eyes open and that million-mile stare, Granny Dwyer seemed content, in a way. I wasn't going to change that. Deep down, I knew CPR wouldn't do her any good. Might make me feel better, brave Jackson O'Connell doing all he could to keep the Angel of Death away. But only for a while. You can't fool yourself for long.

Maybe I'd feel guilty later, and I could do guilt pretty well, having been worked over by nuns and my mom and other professionals in the guilt business when I was young. But right then I decided to just sit beside Granny and hold her hand. She'd just turned seventy-five a few weeks earlier, she had a bad heart, her husband was long gone, kids down in Florida and North Carolina. She'd been lonely the last few years and we'd become good friends.

I opened the front door and put the light on to help the EMTs find the place, then went back and sat with Granny. A prayer seemed appropriate, and I considered the "Our Father" or "Hail Mary" or one of those other ones I'd had to memorize, but they didn't seem right. They didn't mean that much to me anymore. So I winged it.

"Dear God," I said softly, "please take Granny Dwyer into your arms. She was a great person, really kind to me and everyone else. She led a good, caring, and joyous life. Let her have peace. Thanks, God."

Pretty informal, but it seemed appropriate.

The EMTs arrived a minute later. I yelled, "We're in the kitchen!" when I heard them outside the door. A young guy came in first, with an older woman right behind him. They started checking Granny over and asking questions. I told them she had a bad heart, then about how I heard a noise and found her on the floor.

"And then she…died," I said. "She just died."

I expected them to ask me if I tried to revive her, but they just continued their examination. They said something about all her vital signs being negative. The young guy asked, "CPR?" The woman shook her head and said, "Call the coroner."

She stood and walked a few feet away with me. "She's your grandma?"

"No...well, sort of. She's my friend's grandma. A friend of my family. I live with her and take care of her. And she takes—took—care of me." I felt like an idiot, although the woman nodded and seemed to understand.

"Any relatives around?"

"No, they're all out of state. I can call them, if you want."

She patted my shoulder. "Sure...I probably don't have to tell you this, but when you break it to the relatives, be tactful and sensitive. You might want to just tell them that there is an emergency and they should get here quickly. And try to talk to someone who is strong enough to handle the news."

I called Mr. and Mrs. Dwyer in Florida. Would have called Gerry first, but he was traveling in Europe somewhere; he e-mailed me once a week or so, but that was the only way I knew to contact him.

Gerry was Granny's real grandson. He's five years older than me and a good friend, and he was my English teacher until February, when he got caught up in a scandal at school. Gerry said the stink of scandal convinced him it was time to hit the road.

I thought about Gerry while dialing his parents' number. Mr. Dwyer answered the phone, to my relief. Would have been harder to tell Mrs. Dwyer. Maybe something in my voice when I said hello alerted him, because I'd barely started to tell him what happened when he cut me off.

"Is my mother all right?" he asked.

"No, sir, she…died. The EMTs are here. You can talk to them if you want…I'm real sorry, Mr. Dwyer."

He sighed deeply. "That's okay, Jackson. Was it a heart attack?"

"I think so."

"Yeah, she's been getting weaker," he said. "We'll be on a plane tomorrow."

"Would you like me to do anything in the meantime?"

"No, we'll take care of the arrangements when we get there, but thanks for asking."

"I'll e-mail Gerry and let him know, but he might not check it for a few days."

"Good idea. I don't know how else to reach him. Thanks again for calling right away, Jackson. Good night."

"'Night."

Gerry would feel bad if he didn't make it back for Granny's funeral. I got up and sent him an e-mail while I was thinking about it. By the time I was done, the coroner had arrived and had started his exam. He asked me a few questions in the living room. The EMTs made it clear they didn't want me in the kitchen, and I didn't want to go back and see Granny that way.

I sat alone in the living room and thought about Granny and how close we'd become. I could have lived with my mom and sister after my family's meltdown, but they moved to Redbank and I would've had to change schools. Plus, Mom and I weren't getting along that well. She wanted me to side with her in the divorce, tell all the bad stories I had on Dad, but I didn't cooperate. Would have been real tense living with her after that.

When the divorce was going down, I called Gerry to talk about it. He immediately invited me to live with him and Granny, saying they had plenty of room in her house. It was like a door opening but I didn't want to impose, so I said he better check it out with her before he invited me. So he called to her in the kitchen, saying, "Hey Granny, Jackson wants to move in with us so he can keep going to school in Highland. Is that okay?"

"Sure," she called back loud enough that I could hear her over the phone. "You tell Jackson he has a home here anytime he wants."

He also sold his folks on the idea. It was cool, but Gerry told me he had selfish reasons for inviting me, too. He was close to Granny and had taken care of her at the house for a year after his folks retired, even though he really wanted to move out, get a place down at the beach. "I'm in the same bedroom I had when I was five," he told me. "Some of my friends from college moved back home, too, but none of 'em like it. It's not Granny, Jackson, we get along great—it's the house that's freaking me out. Thomas Wolfe was right; you can't go home again."

He'd drop by once a week to have dinner and see how we were doing. And we did fine. Granny became my legal guardian and kept after me about school work. She had rules for me, too, cleaning up after myself and being home at certain hours and all that, but most of the time she was pretty easygoing. She was starting to have trouble driving and her knees bothered her when she walked, so I took her around to places in her car. I teased her that I was "driving Miss Granny."

We also talked a lot, and as we grew closer, I found I could even talk to her about things like my family situation, girls, and the acne army that had invaded and conquered my body. Kind of strange, since I wouldn't even talk to my sister much about stuff like that. With Granny, it was different. I'm not sure why, but I didn't feel like I had to keep up my guard with her. I trusted her completely.

I didn't realize I was crying a little until the guy EMT patted my shoulder. I wiped my face on my sleeve, pretty embarrassed. He explained that they were taking my grandmother to the morgue. I didn't explain the relationship again. It's true that she wasn't my real grandmother— she was much more than that.

TWO

*"He always thought of the sea as la mar
which is what people call her in Spanish
when they love her. Sometimes those who love
her say bad things of her but they are always
said as though she were a woman."*

—Ernest Hemingway

Two nights before the funeral, Gerry flew in from France. I picked him up from the airport in Newark. We shook hands and then he gave me a hug, which made me a little uncomfortable, if you want to know the truth. I'm not much of a hugger.

"Thanks for being there for Granny," he said.

"Hey, she was there for me," I said, feeling my throat suddenly tighten.

I got myself together while we walked down to the baggage claim area. Gerry was always a jock and had an athlete's lean build, but now he was downright skinny. His jeans and T-shirt seemed too loose, hanging on his bones rather than fitting him.

"You hungry, Gerry?" I asked. "We can stop for a bite if you want."

He smiled knowingly. "Yeah, I dropped a few pounds. It's all the walking I've done while traveling around. Why don't we order a pizza when we get back to the house?"

"Good idea." No one ever had to ask me twice if I wanted pizza.

His only luggage was a huge blue backpack. He slung it over his shoulder with ease and we walked to the parking lot, found Granny's brown beast, then drove back to Highland, talking a bit about his trip, otherwise sitting in silence.

Usually I'm pretty sloppy, but I'd made sure Granny's house was perfect. I cleaned everything, even the windows. Gerry seemed pleased and impressed with the condition of the house and the arrangements I'd taken care of, and that made me feel good.

Once the pizza arrived, I teased him as he removed the pepperoni from his half. "Gave up meat," he shrugged. "I should have told you before you ordered. No big deal, just eating down the food chain."

It was good to have him back. I'd really missed him after he took off, even felt a little betrayed, along with the other seniors in his Honors English class. Wasn't logical or anything. We knew what happened wasn't his fault.

Gerry's a cool guy, and only twenty-three. He got dragged to a party at the beach by Marvin Renker and some other seniors. No big deal, he didn't drink or smoke weed or anything, but later this girl lied and said they messed around. She eventually told the truth, but Gerry got in trouble for just going to the party, and Edwards wanted him gone. At Edwards's suggestion, the school board offered him three months severance if he quit in late February, and with all the rumors going around, and his fellow teachers looking at him like he was a creep, he decided to take the offer. He was on a plane to Europe a few days later.

After dinner, we talked about the funeral and reception. Granny left instructions with her lawyer, and he'd given them to me when I dropped by his office in Red Bank. I didn't like the way he looked me up and down like he disapproved of my clothes and age and everything else. He gave me the information, though, and he was obviously fond of Granny, so I stopped thinking about throwing him and his three-piece suit into the Navesink River.

All Granny wanted at her service were some pictures and poems displayed and "a few kind words" from family and friends. Simple and honest, like the way she lived. It took us a few hours to sort through all her photos. The framed ones around the house were almost all formal shots of family, typical boring stuff. The more interesting photos featuring Granny were in four shoe boxes under her bed; three of the boxes were completely filled, the other halfway.

We split up the boxes and selected the pictures we liked best and placed them on the kitchen table, along with some of the poems she'd written and admired. I was a little bored at the beginning, but soon found that I kind of liked sorting through her photographic history, looking back at her life.

They told a story of a loving and adventurous woman. She always looked like she was having fun, especially when she was pictured aboard the family's sailboat. I mentioned this to Gerry.

"Oh sure, you know she was a jock, and sailing was her sport during the middle part of her life, something she could do with the family. I remember sailing around Atlantic Highlands with her and my folks when I was small. She gave it up after Grandpa Ron died. Guess she didn't think she'd get as much enjoyment out of it by herself, and she was getting up in years."

Gerry's grandfather Ron had passed away fifteen years earlier. Granny never talked about her late husband, and I had the impression from little things I'd heard that their marriage was not the best, and part of the reason was her stubborn pride and independent streak. Once, for example, not long after I moved into the Dwyer house, Gerry's father winked at me and said he hoped I found his mother easier to live with than his old man had.

Still, Ron and Marge Dwyer looked happy together aboard their sailboat.

We had piles about six inches high by midnight, and cut them in half by one in the morning. We looked over each other's piles and good-naturedly debated the best of the bunch; our taste was so similar it was kind of scary, like we were brothers or something. We got it down to about twenty photos.

The poems didn't take as long. We picked out one from each of her favorite poets, Emily Dickinson, Robert Frost, and Seamus Heaney; then picked another five of her own poems.

"When she was in her late teens and early twenties, she tried to write one poem a week, and she submitted some of them for publication," Gerry explained as we were sorting. "She got about a dozen published, but stopped writing after she got married. Too busy raising a family and all that. Then she took it up again about eight or nine years ago, and had a few more published. She was proud, although she kept it a secret. She was a little shy about her writing and didn't like to boast. And she thought—correctly—that most people didn't care about poetry and wouldn't want to listen to an old lady talk about that sort of thing."

"We talked about poetry sometimes, but she never mentioned she wrote any herself."

"Probably would have told you eventually," Gerry suggested. "Like I said, she was a bit shy about her writing, and her other accomplishments."

I nodded, thinking about the pictures I'd found of her playing basketball as a young woman. The shy-proud look on her face.

"Granny and my mom inspired my love of literature, to my dad's eternal shame," he continued. "The old man thinks literature is a waste of time, for the most part, maybe something women should take an interest in. He doesn't understand why anyone would want to read poetry or a novel, unless it's one of those techno-thrillers by Tom Clancy."

Granny and Gerry sparked my own interest in books and literature. My parents were not big readers, except for the reading they had to do at work. But when I was around the Dwyer house, his mom and Granny always had books going, not to mention Gerry. He took a speed-reading course when he was a freshman at Rutgers and he could go through books the way I could go through pizza. "It helped my social life," he told me. "The profs pile on the books in college."

Granny and Gerry introduced me to some pretty cool books like *Lonesome Dove* and *Dune* and *Snow Falling on Cedars*, stuff I never would have picked up without their encouragement. All I read were basketball books.

"Take a look at this one," Gerry said, handing over the laminated copy of one of Granny's recently published poems. It was called "Reaching Out":

> *I fling them skyward*
> *Like baseballs into the blue beyond*
> *Trailblazers of the soul*

Propelled by need
Freighted with hope
Uttered with care
Into thin air
Into air

Ask and you shall receive
Seems a little too pat
An electronic teller for
An automated soul
And yet I ask and say thanks
Thy will be done
My will be done
Thy will, my will
Hearts fill and words spill

So toss up another
To Great God, Holy Hero, Dearly Departed
And wait for answers
So often oblique
Sunset and sunrise
Highlights in eyes
Symbols and signs

An old friend told me
She asked for a Benz
I judged her unworthy
And thou shalt not judge
Lest you be judged
Be judged
Begrudged

Mystery of air
Ask this, get that
One from A, two from B
The quiet plea
Sailing worn trails
Above earthly wails
To the blue beyond baseballs

"Wow," I said. "That's really good."

"And not your typical Catholic view of prayer," Gerry noted. "I can't imagine Father Mike appreciating the second stanza, about the Good Lord's words being a little too pat."

"Yeah, probably won't like the Holy Hero part, either," I said.

"Well, like it or not, that one is going to be sitting on a table in the church for everyone to see, and I'm going to read it during the service." His determination gave way to a smile a moment later. "Granny was a rebel, wasn't she?"

I nodded. "A rebel with a heart."

We stood and raised our beverages high. "To Granny," he said grandly.

"To Granny," I repeated. And together we said, "A rebel with a heart."

We clinked and drank. It was after three A.M. and I barely made it to my bed before collapsing in a sleep that lasted until almost noon.

THREE

"I must go down to the seas again,
to the vagrant gypsy life
To the gull's way and the whale's way
where the wind's like a whetted knife;
And all I ask is a merry yarn
from a laughing fellow-rover,
And quiet sleep and a sweet dream
when the long trick's over."

—John Masefield

We buried Granny Dwyer on Wednesday morning. My girlfriend Kelly was there, along with Marvin Renker and my Shoreview buddies Danny Larson, Thaddeus Fly, and Angelo D'Angellini. And I was surprised to see my mother and sister—ol' Mom told me she and Shannon probably wouldn't be able to make it, though she wouldn't tell me why. That pissed me off. I had the feeling she didn't want to go because I'd grown closer to Granny while I grew apart from her.

The weather couldn't make up its mind if it wanted to be sunny or cloudy, and that's sort of how I felt. It was great to see everyone together, and hear the stories of Granny's life, but of course she wasn't able to attend the party.

After Gerry finished reading Granny's poem and saying a few words, it was my turn. From the altar, the gathering looked smaller, like the fans at a track meet, basically. I knew Granny wouldn't have cared. She liked to joke that most of her good friends were dead or wrinkling away in Florida, but I thought it was pretty pathetic. She was the best person I knew and deserved a standing-room-only crowd.

Usually I get nervous when I have to speak in front of people, and a couple of times my voice has broken from the strain. This time, though, I was strangely calm. "I called Marge Dwyer Granny, like just about everyone," I began. "She wasn't my grandmother, although she treated me like a relative. I was just a kid from the neighborhood, playing sports with her real grandson, and she would always make us lemonade, talk to us, and listen to us as if we had something worth saying. We became close friends after everyone moved away, and she really gave me some good advice and guidance. I'll miss her."

Afterward, I looked over the pictures and poems in the back of the church one last time. Kelly came up and put her hand on my shoulder, and I could tell she felt bad for me. When I turned around after silently saying goodbye to Granny, I saw that Kelly was trying to hold back tears. I hugged her for a long time.

I also hugged my sister Shannon, who I could see had been crying, and while I was in this rare hugging mood, I figured I'd give my mom one, too. She looked a little shocked—we hadn't hugged each other in almost two years. I introduced her and Shannon to Kelly, and was proud to add, "my girlfriend."

"Jackson's told me all about you," Mom said, though I really hadn't told her much in our monthly conversations. We usually only checked in with each other and then she'd hand the phone to Shannon. We talked for a while now, and then headed to the reception at the Dwyer house.

On the way, I told Kelly about the conversation Granny and I had a few weeks ago. "I didn't think anything about it at the time, but it seems sort of spooky now because she talked about death. We were reviewing that Shakespeare assignment, remember?"

"The one you turned in late, sure."

"Right. Well, Granny was agreeing with Willie Shakes that life is a play and we're all a bunch of actors, performing our roles. She said we should accept our roles, although it's not always easy. And she said her role was to die soon."

Kelly's eyes went wide. "Yeah, that's a little spooky. And morbid."

"I thought so, but she made it sound like death was no big deal. You know, everybody does it."

After a few moments, Kelly smiled. "I just had a mental

image of Granny walking alongside the Grim Reaper, telling him to cheer up and join the party."

The reception was a little strange. Right off I noticed that sometimes the group was loud and festive, other times quiet and somber. While eating my fill of the spread, I noticed Gerry's parents and went over to say hello, since I'd only talked to them on the phone the last few days. I'd always gotten along okay with Mr. Dwyer, so I was surprised when he hesitated before shaking my hand. Then he gave me a funny look and excused himself.

I shrugged it off and went over to talk to my buddies, who felt a bit uncomfortable around all the older strangers. When they were done eating, I suggested we go and shoot some hoops in the driveway, and they looked relieved. We took off our jackets, rolled up our sleeves, and shot away the formality of the occasion. We talked about graduation parties later that month and plans for the summer. I didn't have any plans myself, which was starting to worry me a bit, not to mention Kelly.

They left a little while later, along with Kelly, my mom, and Shannon. After saying my goodbyes, I shot around by myself. The ball felt good in my hands. After my season ended strongly but a little prematurely, I played a little bit at Danny's famous home court in Shoreview—we call it The High Court—but then got talked into going out for track.

Coach Moran, the basketball coach, actually pitched it to me. I'd started off the basketball season hating his guts because he ruined my plans to be a star, but by the end he'd started playing me much more and sort of admitted that he should have done so from the beginning. I understood by then that he wasn't out to screw me over personally, he was just giving underclassmen playing time to build for the next couple of years, and as a lone senior I was out of luck.

Anyway, he told me to come into his office a few times after gym class, and ragged me about coming out for track, which he also coached. "You can dunk a basketball, O'Connell, so I know you can do at least six feet in the high jump, once you get the technique down. Maybe you can even land a track scholarship, if you're good enough." He knew I was hoping for a basketball scholarship, and he sent the tape of my last game, when I was on fire and scored thirty-two points, around to a few colleges. Two junior college coaches called me and said I could probably walk-on, but I didn't get any scholarship offers.

So I didn't have much going on, other than hanging with Kelly, and she is one of the busiest people in the world. So I went out for track. I was already in shape from basketball, but I started lifting weights for the first time in my life, and my body reacted well to the workouts. I also started working on my flopping technique—short for the Fosbury Flop—every day. I was still perfecting it my first meet, and finished third with a jump of six-feet even. I'd improved a lot since then. Even Moran was surprised at my progress, and suddenly a track scholarship seemed like a real possibility.

Finally I was pumped about something other than basketball. Kelly couldn't believe it. A few days into track season, for the first time in six years, I didn't shoot at least three-hundred shots. In fact, I didn't shoot any. I thought I'd go through withdrawal, and I did a little bit, but not like I was expecting. I'd gone over to The High Court a few times on Sundays and shot with Danny, but it wasn't the same. Angelo was working a job, Thaddeus was rehabbing and playing for an AAU team, and Danny was busy with baseball, so we were all kind of drifting away from the game. I knew this coming summer wouldn't be like last year, when we played games almost every night. Still, I thought I'd start practicing on my own after track was over. I wasn't ready to toss the towel in on my hoop dreams yet, despite the setbacks.

It felt good to hold the leather ball, dribble it, spin it, slap it, and of course shoot it. I hadn't lost my touch, despite the semi-break. Once you really learn to shoot a basketball—and I'd define that as making at least ninety out of one hundred free throws on a consistent basis—you can get the stroke back pretty quick.

Gerry wandered over from the front lawn. I threw the ball to him. He shook his head and tossed it back. "Thanks for taking care of the arrangements," he said. "My folks appreciated it, too. Don't worry about it if they act a little cold toward you, Jax. They got a surprise in Granny's will and are having trouble dealing with it."

I remembered the look Mr. Dwyer gave me. "What's up with the will?" I asked.

"Granny changed it a couple of months ago. She had

her lawyer put in a codicil—an addition—that left you a thousand bucks and her car."

I stopped spinning the ball on my finger. "You're kidding?"

"Nope. And that's why my folks are a bit put out. I think it's great, and told them so, and we ended up yelling at each other. They want to contest the will over that petty point, but they won't. The lawyer's fee would cost more than what she left you."

"It doesn't matter that much to me," I said. "If they want the money and car that bad…"

"No, Jackson. Granny wanted you to have those things, so take them and be thankful." He tossed me the car keys. "Plus, you're gonna need it, buddy. My old man is going to sell this house, and he wants you out as soon as possible. I told him to give you two more days, but that's all I could talk him into."

I felt a little worried. I could stay at my mom's place, but didn't want to. We'd been getting along better, up until she pulled the stunt about maybe missing Granny's funeral. Moving back in with her would be like a step back into childhood. She'd want to treat me like I was still a little kid, boss me around. Danny's place would be much better.

Gerry didn't seem in the mood to shoot around, but he did. Maybe he sensed I was sort of freaked out by everything. "I'm going to be getting an efficiency apartment near here until I head off to grad school," he said.

"You could crash with me, but I'll warn you it's going to be tight with both of us."

"No, I think I'll pack up tonight and stay at Danny's," I said. His girlfriend Rachel had pretty much moved in with him, but I knew he wouldn't mind if I parked in the driveway of The High Court and crashed in my "new" car for a few days until I figured things out. The old brown beast probably had more room than the efficiency Gerry was moving into.

"You sure that would be okay with Danny and his folks?" Gerry asked.

"Yeah, no problem at all."

"Okay, good…Sorry to spring this on you all at once, Jax."

"That's okay. Just tell your folks I had nothing to do with Granny changing her will."

He smiled and nodded. "Didn't want to mention it, but that's exactly what they think. They must be hanging around a bunch of bitter and paranoid people down South, you know? I told them you wouldn't have put Granny up to anything like that, especially for such a relatively measly sum."

"So I might have put her up to it for a larger sum?"

"No, no!" he said before he saw I was smiling. "Got me," he laughed. "Your deductive reasoning and sense of humor are fairly well-developed for a C student."

"Ouch. But anyway, a thousand bucks is not a measly sum to me."

He nodded. "You have any plans for the summer? Work or anything?"

"Not really," I shrugged. "I'm thinking about junior college in the fall, maybe playing ball. So I'm going to want to practice for at least a couple of hours a day. Danny said he might be able to get us jobs working for his dad, but I'm not sure if that will pan out."

"Well, you might have another option," he said. "I saw an old friend of Granny's at the church and had an idea. He's kind of an old bastard, but he might be able to give you a job. Let me go get him."

I could tell he felt bad about what his parents were doing and wanted to make it up to me. Much as I was pissed at his parents, I knew that he was a real friend.

He walked back over with an old guy. The man wore a black suit and tie and would have been as tall as me if he could have straightened his legs, which were extremely bowed. He had a full beard and long gray hair tied in a pony tail. His eyes were an intense blue, which made him look a little pissed himself. He was smoking a cigar when Gerry introduced us. He put it in his other hand to shake.

"Jackson, this is Conrad Dean, a friend of Granny's." His hand was large, strong, and crisscrossed with scars. I said hello and looked him in the eye, but it was hard to hold that glare he had.

"Marge was a good friend to me and my late wife," he said. "I taught her and Ron to sail a long time ago. I understand from young Gerry here that you took care of Granny while he was off roaming the world in search of love and adventure and the meaning of life?" His tone was half-amused and half-critical, but Gerry gave him the benefit of the doubt and chuckled.

"Yes sir," I said. "And Granny took care of me, too."

"All well and good, and I appreciate your sentiment for her...but now you're old enough to look after yourself, right?"

I shrugged, a little annoyed by his tone. "I guess so," I mumbled.

"What's that?"

"I said I guess so."

Conrad Dean glared at me. "Look, kid, Gerry and Marge both liked you, so you must be okay. But if you have something to say, say it loud and clear and don't put your head down."

A flood of anger hit me, and I wondered if old Conrad could catch a basketball rocketed at his face from three feet away. He must have noticed something in my eyes, because he smiled and nodded, as if to say, "Try it, kid." Gerry broke the tension.

"I mentioned to Conrad that you'll need a job and a place to stay soon. He runs a boatyard down at Manasquan and was looking for some help this summer."

"Someone reliable," the old man added. "Went through five young fellas last summer. One lazy, another took off with his girl, one was a thieving..." He seemed to remember the occasion and stopped himself. "They were unreliable," he said. "I pay a good wage for good work, and you can live aboard an old Buccaneer I have at the marina.

All you'll have to pay is the monthly moorage fee—hundred and twenty bucks."

It sounded pretty good, but I wasn't sure I could get along with this guy. They were waiting for an answer, and I didn't want Gerry to think I was an ingrate, so I said—loud and clear—that I'd take the job.

"How much school you have left?" Conrad asked.

"Uh, two and a half weeks."

"So on school days you can get down to Manasquan by, what, four in the afternoon or thereabouts?"

"After this week. I have track practice tomorrow and Friday and a state meet on Saturday."

"Track practice? You a runner or something?"

"No, high jumper."

"Should have guessed, lanky as you are. Being an athlete could help you around boats. Okay, let's make Sunday your first day. You'll work seven to five on weekends, four to eight next week and the week after, and then full-time when you finish school."

"Sounds like full-time now," I murmured.

"What's that?" Conrad snapped.

"Sounds like fun," I said.

He scowled at me. "Work on that direct speech," he said. "See you at seven sharp on Sunday. I liked what you said about Marge at the church."

He walked off with Gerry, who turned and winked at me. I knew he meant well, but I wondered what the hell he'd gotten me into.

FOUR

*"If a man must be obsessed by something, I
suppose a boat is as good as anything, perhaps
a bit better than most. A small sailing craft is
not only beautiful, it is seductive and full of
strange promise and the hint of trouble."*

—E. B. White

A fter the reception, I helped clean up the house, then
got my stuff and packed up the car. Mr. and Mrs.
Dwyer gave me a few dirty looks and didn't say a word.
A little dispute about money and suddenly they were
treating me like a dog. Money can drive people nuts.

I crashed in the backseat of the brown beast at Danny's, as planned, and he said I could crash there all summer if I wanted. I told him I might have a job and place to stay pretty quick, but I'd probably be around for a few days at least.

School was a drag Thursday and Friday—I had a serious case of senioritis. I was excited about heading to Trenton for the state meet on Saturday. Coach Moran said a recruiter told him the minimum height they'd consider would be six-nine, which was just two lousy inches away. Other than the pizza with Gerry, I'd been careful about what I ate the past week and put in good workouts, sprinting, jumping rope, and lifting weights on Monday, Tuesday, and Wednesday, then light jogging and working on my form Thursday and Friday.

Though I was still thinking mostly about Granny, I also did some mental preparation on the bus ride to Trenton. Marvin was quiet, too, and I guessed he was thinking about the perfect shot put. Since it was just the three of us, Coach was driving us in a school van. Now that I had my flopping technique down and was in perfect shape—I'd actually lost six pounds since basketball season—clearing the bar was mostly a mental thing. At the end of practice the last two days, Moran had me put the bar up to seven-seven and had me visualize myself going over it. Six-nine seems fairly easy after you've "seen" yourself clear seven-seven.

Like I said, my technique is the Fosbury Flop, which just about everyone uses now. According to Moran, a guy named Fosbury invented the flop and used it to win the 1968 Olympics. It's only practical if you have a big, soft mat available, since you go over the bar backwards and land on your shoulders. They just had sawdust in the old days, so they would "roll" over the bar chest-first. The advantage of the Fosbury is that you can convert speed into height much more effectively. With a roll, Moran said, you have to slow down quite a bit.

I stretched and jogged a couple of laps to warm up, giving a thumbs-up to Marvin as he loosened his arms in the shot put circle. Nearing the high jump apron, I looked over at my primary competition, a six-foot-six guy named Kevin Jenkins from Newark, who was also a good basketball player. Not quite as good as Thaddeus, but he had Division I offers, I'd heard. Coach said his technique wasn't as sharp as mine, but, he added with a smile, "He can just plain jump higher than you and almost everyone else on the planet."

We both cleared the qualifying height of six feet on our first attempt. Jenkins, I'd noticed, hadn't bothered to remove his sweatsuit. The bar went up one inch at a time after that, and we both passed until it reached six-four. By that time there were only nine jumpers left. A crowd of about one hundred people were gathered around the apron, which is a lot for a track meet.

I cleared six-four with a lot of room to spare and felt I might actually give Jenkins a run for the title. We were the only two left when the bar reached six-seven, and again I cleared my personal best with ease. Jenkins had finally taken off his sweats, but he cleared it with more ease than I did. Then he jogged over to an official and said something. The official came over to me.

"Mr. Jenkins wants to go up to six-nine for the next jump. He's cleared that height before. We can go up to that height, then back down to six-eight if you both miss all three attempts."

"Fine by me," I said, though I wasn't actually as confident as I sounded.

I was excited and ran too fast the first two times, which messed up my steps, and I hit the bar on the way up. Jenkins cleared it on his first attempt and sat watching me nearby. I mentally ran through my steps, told myself to relax, I could do this. I tried not to think about the scholarship or all the eyes on me.

My steps were perfect on my third jump and I soared higher than I ever had in my life. I felt my butt barely graze the bar as I arched over, but it was still up when I landed on the mat. I was about to pump my fist in excitement when I noticed the bar vibrating…and then it fell, and I had to settle for second place.

Coach came right over and hugged me, said he was really proud of my effort and the way I'd improved over the season, which was good to hear. Jenkins was pretty cool, too. He came over and shook my hand and said, "Good jump, man, I thought you had it." Just for kicks, he took a shot at seven-feet and cleared it on his second try, a personal best. Made it look easy. He declined further jumps and Coach Moran and I went over to watch Marvin win the shot put title by almost half a foot.

Coach took us out for burgers afterward, and kept saying

how proud he was. I didn't want to ruin the moment by asking whether my effort might have been enough to get a scholarship. I mean, I barely missed six-nine, I was right there. I'd talk to him about it in a few days.

That night, crashing in the brown beast, I had a freaky dream. I was in a black hole, like a grave, and on top was a high jump bar. The bar kept vibrating and threatening to fall into the hole, and I knew it would kill me. I couldn't move and the vibration would increase, and then a dove would come and sit on the bar and it would stop shaking. It would start shaking again when the dove pushed off to fly away, and wouldn't stop until the dove landed again. Over and over the bar shook and the dove took off and landed, and finally the bird pushed off hard and the bar fell and turned on end and flew down toward my face like a spear and I couldn't move and…I woke up in a sweat, my heart pounding like I'd been sprinting.

I drank some water from the gallon jug I kept in the car and turned on the flashlight I used for reading. The dream had something to do with the high jump, obviously, but also with Granny—maybe she was the dove? Or maybe she sent the dove to keep the bar up? But the dove was a screw-up and nearly killed me instead? I didn't know, but I knew I couldn't go back to sleep, and I knew I'd be a little tired my first day at the boatyard.

.   .   .

Sunday morning I drove over to Manasquan through

a light fog. I found Conrad Dean in his shop near the marina, Dean's Den. It was a neat place filled with nautical equipment. Conrad was sitting on a high stool behind a small counter, typing on a computer with his index fingers. He looked as out of place in front of a computer screen as a Highland High science teacher in a biker bar.

"Just when I think I have this damn thing figured out, it does something that really grieves me," he groused, pounding over and over on one key. He raised his hands as if to give the machine a whack, but reconsidered. He turned his bright eyes to me, and I forced myself to look directly at him this time, although it was hard. He was more intimidating than any basketball player I ever went up against, and some of them could do a pretty good glare.

"How long did you jump?"

"High," I corrected. "I'm a high jumper. I did six-foot-seven."

He gave a single nod but didn't really look impressed. "Win?"

"Second place."

"The first loser."

"I guess," I said, thinking it was a jerky thing to say.

"Don't mean to be rude," he continued, "but as a sailor you learn to look at the cold, hard truth of things. Old habit. Annoys some people, though."

I was about to say something sarcastic but decided to keep quiet. He handed me a set of keys on a ring with a long plastic bobber that advertised his business. "Around the water, O'Connell, you want a key chain that floats," he explained.

"It's huge," I said. "I don't know if that'll fit in my pocket."

"You can probably squeeze it in, but it'll look like you have two packages, if you know what I mean," he said, adding, "that's a joke." He didn't smile at all and it was hard for me to laugh, so I settled for a lame snort-chuckle noise. "I'd recommend getting a small biner and hooking your keys and the float to a belt loop."

"What's a biner?"

"Carabiner." He held his up to show me; it was a little steel contraption shaped like a teardrop, with a hinge on one side. "Mostly carabiners are used by mountain climbers, but they come in handy around the water, too. I sell them for four bucks. Grab one over there and I'll deduct it from your first paycheck."

I did as he said and hooked the keys and bobber to it. I wondered if the bobber would float with all that weight; I'd have to test it later in some clear, shallow water.

Conrad called it quits with the computer and motioned for me to follow him. We went outside into the bright morning sunshine, and he paused to look over the marina and marsh. For a second he looked almost content.

After taking a deep breath of the sea air, he led me to a boatyard behind his shop, and I listened as he gave me an overview of the job. Cleaning boats, repairing boats, painting boats, and, when I'd developed the skills, delivering boats. "Not this summer, I don't think," Conrad said. "You need to develop a respect for the sea and knowledge of boats. Takes a while. You'll never learn everything you need to know, never."

I nodded and looked over the boats in the yard. Mostly sailboats, but there were a couple of powerboats and fishing boats, too. Each had an old tarp below it and was up on stands, with the big sailboats up the highest because of the front and back fins, which I later learned were called the keel and rudder.

"You'll also fill in for me at the office sometimes," he said. "Not much to that, really, just try to answer dumbass questions from weekend sailors and ring up the purchases for 'em."

He gave me a job to occupy me for the day. It involved using an electric sander on the side of a thirty-four-foot Cal sailboat, one of the big ones. I dripped several pounds of sweat onto the tarp, and almost fell off the ladder once. The minutes passed like hours, and I considered telling Conrad to shove the job a few dozen times, even rehearsing the exact phrasing. I could use the money, but would much rather play basketball all summer.

I kept sanding, though, and the day passed. He brought me a tuna sandwich and soda for lunch, then told me to get back to work as soon as I finished. I returned to the sander; I was getting a feel for it and the afternoon went a little faster. As the sun was beginning to set, and I was finishing up a side, Conrad shook the ladder. I didn't see him coming and cussed while grabbing the ladder for balance. This seemed to amuse him—a smile flickered through his beard, then fell away.

"We'll call it a day," he said. "You can finish up tomorrow. Just leave the sander here for the night. The little key opens the yard. Make sure you're here at four sharp. No dilly-dallying after school with your girlfriend."

This was the moment of truth. If I was going to quit, it should be now…I turned to him and said, "I'll be here." Part of me felt like I chickened out, and part of me felt that, hard as it was, this job could be okay. I didn't want to be unreliable like the other guys, but I'd have to wait and see if Conrad was going to be a good boss or a jerk. You usually can't tell on the first day. In any case I shoved my thoughts of quitting onto the sideline for the time being.

Conrad seemed pleased that I'd made a commitment. "When you think you're done sanding the boat, you're not. Believe me. You need to take a slow, careful look around the boat to make sure you didn't miss any blisters, understand? I pride myself in doing a good job. That means you need to do a good job."

I nodded and told him—loud and clear—that I understood.

"You got a touch of sunburn, O'Connell, even being in the shadow of a boat all day. Get yourself some sunscreen from the office tomorrow and, here, wear this from now on." He handed me a goofy-looking hat with a wide brim and a chin tie.

I must have looked skeptical because he suddenly became serious. "This is a sailor's hat. The brim keeps the sun off you, and the string keeps it on your head in high winds. Much better than a baseball cap, and I may have to strike your ass dead if I see you wearing one of those sissy yachting captain hats."

I understood the practicality so agreed to wear the hat. Conrad then told me to get my sleeping bag and anything else I needed for the night from my car. I was figuring that I'd crash in the car at Danny's again, but I was pretty tired and didn't feel like driving the twenty minutes to Shoreview. I grabbed my stuff.

Conrad led me over to the marina, which was surrounded by a high wire fence. He pointed at one of the gates, and I detached the carabiner and turned the key he gave me—and entered a new world.

We walked carefully down the ramp, which was extremely steep. "Low tide," Conrad explained. "This is a floating dock, goes up and down with the tides. It'll be a dozen feet higher when you wake in the morning, and this ramp will have just a slight angle. Amazing, huh?"

"Yeah, that's cool. Is it hard to sleep on a boat with the water going up and down like that?"

He nodded. "You'd think so, wouldn't you? But I've never slept better than on a boat, especially a sailboat. You won't even notice the tide rising and falling until you wake up. The sea will rock you to sleep like a baby."

Down on the dock, I looked around at all the boats

bobbing on the darkening water. I liked the way they looked, although it was hard to explain why. It was sort of like looking at a basketball court for the first time. Something about it just said, "Welcome!"

I followed Conrad down a pier. He took the opportunity to increase my vocabulary, pointing at things on boats and telling me to name it. I knew what a mast was, but he had to tell me that the ropes extending from the boat to the pier are called lines, the front of the boat is the bow, and the back the stern. About halfway down the pier, he turned left onto a narrow extension.

"Finger pier," he said, turning. "And this is your new home."

I tried to hide my disappointment. It was a smallish sailboat that even I could tell was in serious need of repair. The lines were dark and stained and the whole boat was covered with thick green grime. A small blue tarp covered the lower part of the mast and the top of the cabin.

"Looks like it needs some work," I said.

"That she does," Conrad said, stepping aboard. "A boat is always 'she,' not 'it.' That third key on your ring will open the lock on the cabin. I cleaned up belowdecks the other day, but it's up to you to clean the rest of her—and keep her that way. Nothing goes to hell faster than a boat on the water. She's called *Morning Sun*."

"Good name," I said, stepping aboard.

Conrad said, "Sailing etiquette requires that you ask permission to step aboard. I won't come aboard again without asking, and you should get in the habit of doing the same in case you need to go on someone else's boat."

I opened the cabin, pushed back the hatch, and looked inside. Other than some stains on the wall it looked okay. I walked down two steps and nearly hit my head on the hatch.

"You'll have to hunch a little in here, tall as you are," Conrad said. He turned on a reading lamp that was clamped to the side of a counter next to the sink. "I'll let you off tomorrow around six so you can spend a couple hours cleaning her exterior. You'll need to learn a few things before you can do much else here, other than cleaning on a regular basis. On a nice day you can take that tarp off the boom, but get it on if it rains—the hatch leaks in a couple of spots."

I looked around. "So I sleep up there in the bow?" I asked.

"You can. That's the V-berth. May be too tight for you. This kitchen table here folds down and makes a longer, wider berth. That's what I'd recommend, but it's up to you."

"Okay, thanks, Mr. Dean."

"You can call me Conrad, and I'll call you O'Connell and the occasional obscenity, until I trust you, if you reach that point, and maybe even after if you piss me off…One last thing. Here's your homework." He handed me a large book he'd been carrying under his arm. It was called *Sailing Fundamentals*.

"Read two chapters a night, and when you're finished,

read it again. Then I'll give you another book. 'Night, O'Connell. Four sharp at the yard."

"'Night, Conrad."

While I set up the bunk, I noticed small movements of the boat. I'd slept in a tent, a treehouse, and a car, but this was my first night on a boat. It was getting cool, so I crawled into my sleeping bag, opened the book, and began learning about my new world.

FIVE

*"Many beginning sailors find themselves
in irons. The term means that the boat is
stopped, pointing directly into the wind, having lost all headway. It will not sail off on
either tack...It happens to everyone at one
time or another. Just be patient. Relax."*

—Gary Jobson

The next couple of weeks were Stephen King strange. I missed Granny of course and felt really down some days; it sounds cold, but a few times I forgot that she was dead. I'd be anxious to tell her about working at the boat-yard, all the interesting things, and then I'd remember that she wasn't around.

I was also finishing my undistinguished high school career. Like the other seniors, I found myself looking back over the last four years with both fond and not-so-fond memories. I'd say it was a toss-up, but might have been on the positive side if I'd gotten a scholarship.

Coach Moran broke the news to me before I went to his office. He found me at a table during lunch and motioned for me to follow him to a hallway. If he had really good news, he probably would have told me in front of Marvin and the other guys.

"I called all the college coaches I know," he said, "and told them that you could clear six-nine, you barely missed it, and finished second in the state meet. They all said to tell you congratulations, but...none offered a scholarship. The line is that they'd love you to attend, you could walk-on freshman year, and if you did well they could get you a scholarship after that."

I nodded and shook his hand. "Thanks, Coach. I'll think about it. I was hoping for a full-ride, you know, basketball or track or a combo, so I'm not sure what I'm going to do. Thinking junior college, probably. My grades are just so-so, and I don't have the money to pay for a four-year school."

"Well, don't get down, Jackson. You're the second best high jumper in the state, for crissake, and a helluva good basketball player. Stay positive."

I thanked him again. He'd really worked hard for me, and pushed me in a good way. Unbelievable that I thought he was such a jerk at the beginning of the year. It made me question how much going on in my life was real and how much was my thinking shoving its way into reality.

I didn't tell Coach that between school, Kelly, the boat-yard job, and a little hoops practice, I didn't have much time to stay positive or get depressed. It was just go, go, go.

The only time I thought about the end to my high school sports career was late at night aboard *Morning Sun*. For almost my whole life I'd been a jock. I'd worked out or played some sort of sport just about every day, and like I said, for the last six years I hadn't missed a day of basketball. So I'd be reading the sailing book in my bunk, trying to focus, and suddenly I'd get an urge to just play. Usually I'd sit up and shoot a couple dozen imaginary jumpers. The shot motion was so ingrained in my body I couldn't get rid of it. Plus, I wasn't burning the motion out of my system with big practice sessions. Shooting hoops was part of my body and soul, and wasn't going away any time soon.

Sometimes I felt the need for a real workout, so I threw on my sweats and ran along the beach, sprinting sometimes, then faking and flying past imaginary defenders and dunking or pulling up for a J. The thunder of the waves sounded sort of like the thunder of applause when I played well, and I'd bow to the ocean. Wish the real applause had been more frequent in high school. Maybe it would be in college, if everything fell into place.

I could tell Kelly was trying to be patient. She was so driven and focused it was difficult for her to have a boyfriend who didn't know what the hell he was going to do after the summer, not to mention with the rest of his life. We'd known each other since sixth grade, but didn't start going out until almost halfway through this year. I was shy because of my acne and didn't think any girls noticed me, except maybe to be grossed out. But Kelly worked on the school newspaper with me, and she was in the English honors class with Gerry, and we just sort of clicked after a while.

I told Kelly I loved her during my last game of the season. Sort of funny, because it was at the end of the best game of my life, and she asked me later to repeat the statement. "I want to make sure it wasn't a combination of adrenaline and the zone you were in talking," she said. So I told her again. And she said she loved me, too. And we had something fantastic for a few months.

Maybe we still did. I know I still loved her, and looked forward to talking to her and looking into her big brown eyes every day. But lately she'd been a little distracted. She's getting ready to go to Princeton, and I know she's excited about that. I'm excited for her. She just can't return the favor because I'm in boatyard limbo right now. She thinks I should find something to be passionate about besides basketball. She's right, as usual, but it pisses me off when she starts talking about my life "beyond basketball."

Because of Granny passing away, Kelly was in support mode when I saw her, which wasn't all that often. She'd more or less graduated from community college through this "Running Start" program, and as a result she was rarely around Highland High. And I headed to the boatyard right after school.

Anyway, with all this going on, I was exhausted. I went

to a party with Kelly on Saturday after my first week of work, and fell asleep an hour later in a hammock in the backyard. She graciously let me sleep, but Marvin sprayed me with the garden hose to wake me up when the party was winding down.

I dreamed that I fell overboard and was drowning, and woke up soaking wet on the grass next to the hammock. Everyone was laughing. Kelly helped me up and explained what happened, struggling not to laugh herself. For a minute I was mad at Marvin. Anyone else did that and we might have had a fist fight. It's hard to be pissed at Marvin, though, because he's just a goof who likes to have fun. Plus, he's huge and a great athlete. He's the same height as me—six foot three—but weighs seventy pounds more and is an All-State linebacker in addition to being the shot put champ. You think twice about getting into it with a guy like Marvin Renker.

I had trouble staying awake at school, too. Living aboard the boat in Manasquan, I had to get up an hour earlier than usual to get to school on time, which didn't help. I would have blown off my first period statistics class if possible, but I needed to pass in order to graduate, and I currently had a D. I liked the teacher, Mr. Winters, and I enjoyed calculating basketball stats, so I had a basic understanding of the subject. The problem was that I ignored the dull assignments and most of the homework.

Mr. Winters was annoyed when I fell asleep in class a few times during my tired days. He'd drop a textbook on my desk to wake me up. I always apologized and tried to stay alert by sneaking sips of the caffeine-loaded soda in my backpack, but sometimes my desk naturally became a pillow. I didn't even remember consciously putting my head down, it just ended up there.

On the last Friday of my high school career, I had three final exams. The only one I needed to pass in order to walk in graduation the next week was statistics. I was done with the test pretty quickly and actually checked over my work. I thought I did okay.

After handing in my exam, I went back to my desk and fell asleep. Mr. Winters liked it quiet as a tomb during tests, so I knew he probably wouldn't disturb me.

I was wrong. He shook me awake about ten minutes later. "You were snoring, Jackson!" he said. "Snoring!"

"He was drooling, too," said a girl next to me, clearly grossed out. The rest of the class started laughing, but Mr. Winters silenced them by saying "Quiet!" in a whispered yell. He always had firm control of the class.

He motioned for me to follow him into the hall. Normally he wouldn't have left the room during a test; only a few students were still working, though, and they weren't sitting close enough to cheat.

"Jackson, I know you're at the end of your high school career, but you need to stay awake in my class," he said. He was standing so he could see the class through the narrow window in the door.

"Sorry, Mr. Winters."

"You're not the most dedicated student I've had, but you've never been disrespectful before."

"Disrespectful?" I asked. "I'm not being disrespectful."

"You don't think you show disrespect—not to mention set a bad example—when you put your head down and snooze away when I'm trying to teach you and the rest of the class?"

"Yeah, okay, I see what you mean," I said. "I'm just really tired. I can't help it."

"Ah, you mean you're required to attend senior parties until all hours?" he asked. "That's something you simply can't control?"

"Hey Mr. Winters, you're jumping to the wrong conclusion," I said, a little angry. "I haven't been going to parties, I've been working."

He looked me over slowly, seeming to notice my combination tan-burn for the first time. "Outdoor work, I take it?"

"Yeah, at a boatyard in Manasquan."

"I thought you'd been partying and working on your tan."

"I wish. It's hard work and I'm putting in forty hours a week, not counting the homework my boss gives me."

"Well I hope you're at least completing his assignments," he said with a little smile. "What kind of homework do you need to do at a boatyard?"

"Part of the job is delivering sailboats, so I'm learning to sail," I said. "I finished two books so far—and I had to read them twice."

He smiled again. "I sail a bit myself. Just for pleasure now with my family, but I crewed on some racing boats in college."

"Cool," I nodded, although I had trouble picturing Mr. Winters, with his portly build, moving quickly around a sailboat.

"Did you know there's quite a bit of math involved in sailing, Jackson?"

"Uh, not really."

"Oh, sure. To navigate effectively you have to understand how to calculate knot speed, tides, current, and of course the distance you plan to cover. Time is another factor you work in with a formula. You have to triangulate to find your position using landmarks. And to anchor you need to know ratios in order to have the proper scope."

The terms rang a faint bell. I'd come across them in the books Conrad gave me, although I just had the vaguest understanding. I'd have to go back over that material.

Mr. Winters gave me a little start when he realized how long we'd been in the hall. He flung open the door and hurried inside, nervously checking his watch, directing a couple of students to sit down, collecting the remaining tests. I probably could have walked off and had a nap on a bench outside without him noticing—but that would have been really disrespectful.

SIX

"If you have crossed the Atlantic in a small boat, say, 'I do a little sailing.'"

—Andre Maurois

Graduation was kind of a letdown. Granny had been excited about it, but with her gone, it wasn't anything special. Gerry was there, but I could tell he felt a little uncomfortable among his former colleagues. A few came up beforehand, when he was talking to me and Kelly, and asked him what he'd been doing since he—ah-hem—left Highland. He told them he'd been bumming around Europe. They nodded with faraway stares and said that was great, good to see you, take care.

"A few of them told me taking off for Europe was a great idea, that it would make me a better teacher in the long run," he said. "But most of the staff looked at me like a guy who might have rolled in the hay with a female student."

Kelly wasn't enjoying the pomp and circumstance, either. She'd finished with a perfect grade-point average and was the real valedictorian for our class, but the honor was taken away by Principal Edwards because of a prank she and I pulled off with the school paper. The prank made him look bad, which wasn't hard. He'd promised Gerry that Kelly would be valedictorian, but after he took off for Europe, Edwards told her no, that he'd changed his mind, she didn't deserve the honor. She called him names and stormed out of his office, and even though her dad had some pull with the school board, he stuck by his decision.

She'd been upset about it for the last few weeks, and I saw she'd been crying when I went to her house to pick her up for graduation. Kelly's last name is Armstead, so she was in the front row for the ceremony on the football field, and even from six rows back I could tell she was having trouble during the speech by the newly appointed valedictorian, Jane Shepherd.

Kelly was annoyed that Jane hadn't talked to her about the situation, just acted like she deserved the honor all along. After Jane said, "I put in many hours and made many sacrifices in order to be your valedictorian," Kelly turned and looked at me with her jaw set in a homicidal expression. Her pretty brown eyes seemed to turn coal black with bitterness.

When Principal Edwards handed me my diploma, giving me a fake smile, I decided to have a little revenge for Kelly's sake. So I smiled back and tried to crush his hand. My hands aren't really that big for a guy my size, so to compensate I squeezed rubber balls and did grip flex exercises every day for years. They'd gotten even stronger working at the boatyard, and I had Edwards in agony in less than two seconds. I released his hand when he opened his mouth to scream, and I saw him look down and shake it to get the blood recirculating. There was nothing he could do to me now—I was free.

Kelly was in a much better mood when I found her on the field after the hat throwing. "You almost made him cry!" she yelled above the din. "Jackson, I was so proud!"

I kissed her, and told her I loved her, and she told me the same. My Shoreview friend Angelo was getting married in a week, and I would have married Kelly the week after if she'd have said yes. I knew she didn't want to get married, though. She was going off to Princeton, and I was going off somewhere else, as yet to be determined. We both knew that whatever I did, it was going to be far less impressive than Princeton.

We talked for a while on the football field with some classmates and well-wishers. Gerry congratulated us and gave me a present and several cards. The present was from him—a copy of *The Oxford Book of the Sea*. His card said, "For my friend Jackson, wishing you fair winds and fantastic adventures." I was touched. I really didn't know if I'd develop an interest in sailing and the sea beyond my summer job, but Gerry seemed to think I was heading in that direction.

Another card contained a picture of Granny and a thousand-dollar check, the money she left me. "I've had it almost a week but decided to hold it for the occasion," he said. "Hope you don't mind."

"No, that's fine," I said. I silently thanked Granny, looking at her smiling face in the picture. My Dad also sent a card, along with a check for two hundred. He'd written me about six weeks before on stationery from his new firm in Los Angeles, asking for the details of graduation because he was planning to attend. I told Mom, and she said sorry, but she and Shannon couldn't handle seeing him, so they wouldn't be coming.

As it turned out, I'd had a call at Dean's Den from Mr. Dwyer a couple of days before. He said my father had called and told him he wouldn't be able to make graduation because he had a big project to work on. "Gerry picked up your mail," he added. "Get your new address and phone number to your father and everyone else you know. I don't want people trying to contact you here anymore."

I was tempted to mouth off with something smart, but because he was Gerry's father, I let it go. I suppose I could have called Mom and told her about the new development, but I knew she'd just gloat about what a jerk Dad was, and I didn't want to hear it.

Sort of funny, Mom's card included a check for $250—like she knew how much Dad sent me and wanted to top it.

I didn't dwell on that, because suddenly I had almost fifteen-hundred bucks in my pocket, which was more money than I'd ever had at one time in my life. I felt nervous with all those checks, and felt like I should get over to the bank and open an account. Gerry said he had to get going before anymore well-meaning ex-colleagues made him feel like a slacker for bumming around the world when he should have been working and fighting injustice. I thanked him again and said I'd talk to him soon.

Kelly's family had surrounded her while I was talking to Gerry. She introduced me to a few of her relatives who came in from out of town. She'd say, "This is Jackson," not, "This is my boyfriend." Maybe the boyfriend thing was implied.

Her mom gave me a hug and congratulated me, and her father and I shook hands. I could tell it was an effort. While her mom liked me, her dad was lukewarm on the best of days. He made it clear that he didn't think I was good enough for Kelly, and held a grudge about a time I'd stupidly blown her off when we were supposed to go to a dance. I thought he should get over the grudge, but I more or less agreed with him about my dull place in her bright universe.

We followed them back to the Armstead house for a

cookout. Kind of felt like I was barging in on a family reunion, but everyone was friendly. The only problem was that they all felt compelled to ask me about my future. It started with Mr. Armstead, who sat in the wicker chair next to me when I was polishing off my second cheeseburger. "So Jackson," he said, "what are your plans now?"

"Well, I'm working in a boatyard down at Manasquan for the summer," I said, wiping the ketchup from my mouth. "And I'm thinking about community college." That last part wasn't exactly a lie—I was thinking about community college. Sort of as a last resort, but I was thinking about it.

Mr. Armstead was nodding but I could tell he was unimpressed. "Sounds like a fine plan. What are you going to study?"

"To be honest, I really haven't decided," I said. "I thought I'd take a few general courses and figure it out from there."

More nodding and then a slight smile. "You know, Kelly has almost enough college credits to have an associate degree already, along with her diploma."

"Yeah, pretty wild. I know she'll do great at Princeton."

"Yes, I'm sure she will, although I think it will be a challenge at first. It's quite a jump from high school and community college to the Ivy League. She's going to need to focus her first year, be free of outside distractions."

He had one particular distraction in mind, I figured.

"Well, you kids have fun tonight," he said. "Jackson,

I know you'll be out late at parties, but I want Kelly home by two a.m. And I want you to watch the drinking. I know you've been responsible on other occasions, but I feel compelled to remind you tonight."

"Not a problem, Mr. Armstead. I have to work early tomorrow morning, so I'm not going to drink anything tonight."

"Good man," he said, patting my shoulder. He went to get some food, to my immense relief. We left a few minutes later. Kelly was over her anger and soaring along on a natural high, so I didn't think it was a good time to bring up stuff about our relationship.

The parties were okay, although I'm not much of a party guy. Highland has a lot of rich people, and some of them can be snotty. I really don't care a whole lot about money and status and all that stuff. I mean, I felt like a king with fourteen-hundred-plus in my pocket.

Even Kelly gets caught up in that status thing sometimes. At the first party, she didn't want me to park the brown beast behind the other, much nicer cars that were pulling up. She insisted that I park out of sight a block away.

While I was sipping sodas, Kelly drank enough for both of us. One minute I saw her putting away a beer, the next downing a shot of Jack Daniels, then holding some kind of mixed drink. On the way to the second party, she was talking a mile a minute about nothing and everything. I'd noticed before that drunks can get into pretty good conversations with themselves. "Kelly," I said, trying to get her attention. "Kelly!" I repeated when she ignored me. Finally I yelled, "KELLY!" She stopped talking and looked at me with a deer-in-the-headlights stare.

"God, Jack...Jackson, you don't to shh-yell."

"Kelly, you're drunk. Why don't you lighten up and just drink soda with me at the next party?"

"Oh, it's graduation!" she laughed. "It's party time! Don't y-you worry, cutie, I'm fur-fine." She leaned over and kissed me hard, looking anything but fine and blocking my view of the road. I had to slow down and get her back on her side of the car.

The second party was more of the same. Kelly ignored my advice for an hour, and then she disappeared for a while. At both parties I found myself in conversations that revolved around the theme of the evening, The Future.

"Boatyard for the summer, thinking about community college," I said the first dozen times. When that got old I started saying, "I don't have a clue!" which was closer to the truth. Naturally I asked about their plans, and my classmates went into much more detail. I heard about every college on the East Coast. I heard about more majors than we have in the Army, Navy, and Air Force combined.

An hour later I found Kelly kneeling on the floor of the bathroom, hair in her face, riding the porcelain bicycle. I cleaned her up, struggled her to the car. Her only conversation this time was to shout, "Pull over!" She said this three times, and I think she emptied her stomach entirely on the final vomit stop. I drove to a convenience store for water and some food. She drank the water but almost puked again when I offered her a cookie.

Naturally, I didn't want to take her home in this condition, but it was closing in on the deadline. I was tempted to sit her on the front porch, ring the doorbell, and run like hell. I felt guilty even though it wasn't my fault. Kelly is smart and strong-willed and does what she wants.

I got her inside with her key, straining to keep her and the process quiet. No such luck. As I was walking her upstairs to her room—slowly and carefully, she had no balance—her father stepped out of the master bedroom wearing pajamas and a scowl. "What the hell is going on?" he hissed.

"She had too much to drink," I said, thinking it was pretty obvious.

He came over and helped me guide her up the last few steps and to her room. At the door he turned and said, "I knew I couldn't trust you, O'Connell. You're no good for her, never have been. Get out of my house."

More or less what I expected, but that didn't make it any easier to hear. I could explain my innocence the rest of the night and it wouldn't do any good. I drove back to Manasquan trying to forget about my graduation night. Most of it, anyway. Every now and then I pulled the checks out of my wallet to smile at them again. And I said a little prayer of thanks to Granny.

SEVEN

"A solitary sail that rises white in the blue mist on the foam—what is it in far lands it prizes? What does it leave behind at home?"

—Mikhail Lermantov

I was tired Saturday morning, and grateful that Conrad gave me a relatively easy job—tearing the upholstery out of one of the sailboats up on stands. It was another hot day and I rigged up a small fan with extension cords so I wouldn't suffocate in the interior of the boat.

As was his habit, Conrad knocked on the hull when he wanted my attention around noon. "O'Connell, let's have some lunch," he said. "I'm giving you the rest of the day off."

"All right," I said, tossing aside the carpet I was holding and turning off the fan. "What's the occasion?"

"You graduated from high school yesterday, right? That's cause for celebration, I suppose."

We ate at one of the nicer fish houses down at the port. Conrad asked me about the ceremony, though I could tell he really didn't care. I mentioned Kelly and the late parties and the fact that I'd pissed off her father. "Nice looking girl," Conrad said, munching on his halibut burger. "Remember her from the funeral service. So she's going off to the Ivy League and her old man doesn't like you."

"Yeah, that about sums it up. He doesn't think I'm good enough for her, which might be true, but it kind of pisses me off." Usually I didn't talk so much about what I was really thinking and feeling. I was tired from being up late and working hard through the morning, so my guard was down. And for some reason I trusted Conrad, even though he could be a pain sometimes.

"You're going to meet a lot of his type if you stay around here," Conrad said with a nod. "Bluebloods who think they own the whole damn world. Sailing can be done on the cheap, O'Connell. But there's always been an arrogant segment of the sailing population. They own the fancy boats and the latest electronics, and their floating cocktail parties outnumber their sea-going voyages about twenty to one.

Ignore them as best you can. You've probably seen them at the Den."

"Yeah, that afternoon I covered for you," I recalled, "a guy came in and snapped his fingers at me, then told me to get a cart and follow him. He tossed stuff back over his shoulder without looking. I had to catch it and put it in the cart. I was thinking about clubbing him on the back of the head with the wooden tiller he threw at me, but I didn't think you'd appreciate it, considering that he bought almost four-thousand bucks worth of stuff."

Conrad snorted and almost smiled. "I thought you'd screwed up when I saw the receipts, O'Connell. A week's worth of sales in one afternoon. Happens every now and then. If that ass wants to spend a bundle in my shop, I guess we'll let him live, right?"

Conrad paid for lunch and we returned to the boat-yard. He tossed me the keys to his pickup and told me to hook up the "little fella," which is what he called the *Sunfish* sailboat he kept on a trailer in a corner of the yard. "Give me twenty minutes to close down the Den for the day," he said.

I was a little surprised because a fair amount of people were wandering around the marina area, all potential customers. For weeks he'd been telling me that he'd show me the ropes on the *Sunfish* some day, after I'd read a few sailing books and understood the basics. I was pleased the day had arrived. Pleased and a little nervous.

After I hooked up the trailer, I sat in the shade to wait.

Then my phone rang. Conrad gave me an old cell phone he had earlier in the week, saying he hated the damn things but they came in handy when you were living on a boat. I'd only given the number to Kelly, Danny, and my dad so far, and if I knew Danny, he was at graduation parties until dawn. In fact, he might still be celebrating.

"Hey Kelly," I answered, "I wanted your body last night but you were too hammered. How's the hangover?"

Silence for a few deadly seconds. "This is Mr. Armstead, Jackson," her father said. I winced and felt the blood drain from my face. "Kelly has assured me that you were not responsible for her condition last night, and in fact tried to talk her out of drinking so much. I suppose...I owe you an apology. Here's Kelly."

He handed the phone off before I could accept the apology or try to lamely talk around the foot in my mouth. "Hey you," Kelly said in a sleepy voice. "I feel like someone beat me up."

"Sorry to hear that, Kels. You were pouring them down one after the other. You seemed to be trying to set a record."

"Yes, the drunkest valedictorian-should-a-been. Look, I know it's an egotistical hang-up on my part, but the injustice of the situation made me an emotional wreck. I mean, for the rest of my life I'm going to have to explain that I wasn't valedictorian of my school because I wrote a righteous editorial on a lost cause."

"Hey, it was a great editorial and a just cause. And who do you have to explain it to?"

She took a deep breath. "You're right, Jackson. I don't have to explain to anyone. But I was still hurt over the situation, and I guess I needed to turn out my lights last night."

"There was a definite Kelly power outage in the greater Highland area."

"Thanks for putting up with me."

"Thanks for straightening out your dad."

"I have a vague recollection of him blaming you and ordering you out of the house. I'm so sorry. I explained that it was all my fault when I woke up a half hour ago. He was still ranting."

We made plans to see each other on Tuesday evening and said goodbye. Having just gone from frying pan to fire with Mr. Armstead, I wondered what kind of reception I'd get. I was sure he'd spend some time thinking over my unthinking comment.

Conrad emerged from the Den and locked up the building. He turned the OPEN sign around. It read CLOSED or SAILING.

He slid into the passenger seat. I followed his directions to the public boat launch over at a small inlet. "Best to learn here before you venture out into the ocean wild," he said as he opened the door. "You turn around and back the boat down into the water. Go slow, watch me in your mirror."

"Okay, sure."

I got the truck turned around on the second try; the

first time I turned too sharply and the boat was suddenly alongside the truck rather than behind it.

"Turn the wheel in the opposite direction you want the boat to go!" Conrad shouted, drawing the attention of a couple dozen sunbathers. "The opposite direction, O'Connell!"

Embarrassed, I just wanted to get the boat in the water as quickly as possible. I started backing toward Conrad again, but after a few feet the trailer began fading to the right. I spun the wheel the other way, the trailer straightened out for a moment—then turned sharply to the left. I looked up at Conrad in the rearview mirror. His face was red with anger, the way I'd seen him a few times when I'd screwed up jobs at the yard.

"Pull forward!" he yelled. "Pull the damn truck forward and straighten her out!" This was followed by a stream of obscenities. A woman on the beach shouted, "I have small children over here, mister!"

"My apologies, ma'am," Conrad said. "I have a moron driving my truck."

That got a few laughs from the crowd. Now I was red in the face. When Conrad went off on me, he reminded me of my father. Dear ol' Dad used to have me help with projects around the house just so he'd have someone to yell at. He usually called me stupid idiot, while Conrad's term of affection was damn moron. Maybe that was progress.

I stopped the truck and took some deep breaths. I was really hot and wanted to punch his lights out. I hate to admit it, but part of me was also ready to back down, try to pretend that it wasn't happening, get it over with as quickly as possible.

But I'd learned a few things about bullies over the years, from my father and various Putdown Predators. I learned that you have to call the bluff on bullies, even if you're scared of getting your butt whipped. I knew Conrad couldn't whip me, although he could fire me...well, I could get another job.

I stepped out of the truck as Conrad walked up alongside. "What the hell are you doing?" he yelled, getting in my face. "I said straighten the truck out! Christ, if I'd have known you were such a damn moron, I never would have hired you!"

I grabbed him by his shirt, turned him quickly, and shoved him against the truck door. He was stunned for a second, then angry. He struggled but I pinned him hard. Although he smoked cigars and never worked out, he was pretty strong for his age, and I could tell he was surprised that I'd lifted him a couple of inches off the ground and he couldn't do a thing about it.

"Let me go!" he shouted, blue eyes on fire and yellow teeth snapping like a Doberman.

"First you listen. I appreciate the job and place to stay, but I'm not going to take your crap anymore. You call me a moron again, I'm gonna punch your lights out. You want to fire me, go ahead."

I released my grip, took a step back, and readied for

a counterattack. He was still snarling and maybe thinking about it. I looked right into those hard, bright eyes of his—they weren't intimidating anymore. When I saw that he wasn't going to take a swing at me, I expected him to fire me. I liked the job, the money, the nautical education, and my home on the water. And I was prepared to give it all up.

He straightened up, ran a hand through his gray beard. "Go down to the ramp and direct me," he said softly. "I'll back her down."

I nodded and walked toward the ramp. A few guys on the beach had stood up, and everyone was looking at us. The Conrad and Jackson show. I tried to ignore the stares.

He pulled far forward until the boat was perfectly straight. Then he backed toward me, making it look pretty easy. I waved him along and put up my hand in a stop signal when the *Sunfish* was floating. I released the bow from the trailer and signaled Conrad to pull ahead. No parking places were nearby, and he had to park a couple hundred yards away.

Rigging the *Sunfish* was relatively easy. I unfurled the sail from the mast and pushed it into the round hole on the deck. Then I realized that the boom—the horizontal bar that holds the sail on the bottom—needed to be attached to the mast first. I removed the mast, slid it through the hole at the end of the boom and back into place. I snapped the rudder and tiller into the holes in the stern as Conrad walked up.

He inspected my work and grunted his approval, then

gracefully pulled himself into the cockpit. I shoved us off and hopped aboard, somewhat less gracefully. He inserted the centerboard into the slot slowly, making sure we had enough depth so it wouldn't scrape along the bottom.

"Centerboard keeps the boat moving forward instead of laterally when the wind hits the sail," he said. "The small boat version of a keel."

I nodded, although I knew that much. He knew I knew that much. Talking was better than silence right then.

Conrad had me take the tiller while he raised the sail. "Always check the wind direction first," he said, "otherwise you could end up in the water real quick." He had me change direction slightly before he yanked on the line. "What am I pulling on?" he said.

"Uh, the sheet?"

"Incorrect. This is the halyard. The sheet is the line that controls the mainsail. Once you get the sail raised, back it off an inch, then tie the halyard to this cleat here." He tied it off in a figure-eight so quickly it was hard to follow.

"Let's switch now." Staying low, we moved past each other. He grabbed my forearm for balance briefly, and gave a little squeeze and winked as our eyes met. I smiled and nodded.

He had me untie the halyard and retie it to the cleat six times, until I could do it fairly fast. "A little thing, but crucial," he said. "Practice it on *Morning Sun*. You should be able to tie a line to a cleat in your sleep."

We were well away from shore, and the curious faces

of the beach crowd faded into the distance. The wind picked up. Conrad had me take the tiller while he held the sheet, showing me how to "read" the sail and let the sheet in or out for maximum efficiency.

A half-hour later he handed me the sheet and made himself comfortable beside the centerboard, at least as comfortable as you could be on such a small boat. He took me through the points of sail, which I understood pretty well. Basically, you couldn't sail directly into the wind. You had to tack back and forth to reach a point toward the wind. You moved best when the wind was off to the side—a beam reach, I think it was called—although you lost speed if the boat heeled over too far. Running with the wind was my favorite. I liked the way it sounded, like going with the flow of everything, even though it wasn't that fast. To run you let the sail way out, to catch the wind from behind the boat. And you watched carefully so you didn't jibe, which was when the boom shoots violently to the other side. Conrad told me to keep my head down and did an intentional jibe. Even the small boom on the *Sunfish* might have knocked me out and maybe overboard during a jibe.

Every few minutes Conrad ordered a change of direction. "When the wind is in front, use the come about stunt," he said. "When the wind is behind, keep a jibe in mind."

"And if you can't tie a knot," I added, "tie a lot."

He snorted and almost chuckled. "Practice your knots and practice with this little fella anytime you want," he said. "Tell you what, O'Connell. You have enough room in your slip to keep her moored alongside *Morning Sun*. So drop me off on shore in a while, then sail up the river and back to the marina by yourself. Be a good test for you."

"Okay, Conrad…Thanks, this is a great graduation present."

"You're welcome. You have a good feel for the boat. Learn the small boat well, then you can move up in size. That's how you learn to sail."

He looked overhead at some gulls hanging almost motionless on the breeze. We sailed along in a better silence, both enjoying the feel of the wind on our faces and the simple movement of a boat across the water. After another half-hour, Conrad sighed. "I should get back to the Den and make some money. Bring her about, O'Connell, and take me back to the ramp."

"Aye-aye, Skipper," I said. "Prepare to come about."

He almost smiled.

EIGHT

*"To reach the port of heaven, we must sail
sometimes with the wind and sometimes
against it—but we must sail, and not drift,
nor lie at anchor."*

—Oliver Wendell Holmes

"What do you need with a baseball bat?" Kelly asked, looking at the thirty-six-inch Louisville Slugger in the backseat of the car.

"It's required," I answered. "Check the invitation if you don't believe me. Some events are black tie, this one is big bat."

"A bat at a wedding?"

"Well, it's baseball season. If it was January, I'm sure basketballs would have been required."

We were on our way to the wedding ceremony of Angelo D'Angellini and his girlfriend Debbie Franco. She was only sixteen, just finished her sophomore year, but was dropping out to work and get a GED. Kelly guessed she was pregnant, that's why they were getting married so young. Angelo hadn't said anything about that to me, and I sure as hell wasn't going to ask him about it.

Kelly was wearing a smart and sexy light blue dress and matching pumps that put her eye level with me. I had on my only suit and tie, the same outfit I'd worn to prom and graduation. I explained to Kelly what a sacrifice it was for me to wear a formal outfit.

"That's fine, Jackson, I know you're an informal kind of guy," she said. "Although I must say you shine up pretty well. Especially with that new beach tan. Your skin is looking really good. And your hair is a little lighter, too."

"Thanks. The sun gets you if you're outside all day, even with a hat."

"So what did you guys do at the bachelor party last night?"

"Nothing too wild. We shot hoops at The High Court. Probably for the last time, at least with all of us together."

"Life moves on," she shrugged.

"Yeah, that's true, but playing ball with those guys meant something, you know? It was a big part of my life."

"I wasn't belittling the experience," she said, rubbing my forearm affectionately. "But it was time for you to light out for new horizons. You can't spend the rest of your life shooting hoops in the driveway."

"Be a good job if you could make some bank," I said. "Maybe I should print up business cards. 'Jackson O'Connell, Driveway Hoop Specialist.'"

"I don't think there's a big market for that," she said, then gave me her Kelly look. This involves her chin tilting forward, a frown, and hard stare of her big brown eyes. "You rather slyly changed the subject on me. So that's all you guys did was shoot hoops?"

"Well, later we dropped by a strip club where Danny knows this guy, but we didn't inhale."

"Very funny."

"Honestly, Kelly, strippers don't do much for me," I protested. "It's like the cookie jar is right in front of you but you're not allowed to have any."

"You better not be having any cookies as long as you're with me, buster."

"You know you're the only girl I like to see naked."

She gave me a little slap on the face, not very hard. "I'm a young woman, not a girl," she said. "And don't you forget it."

To my surprise, neither Kelly nor her father had said anything about my stupid remark on the phone. I'm sure she would have mentioned the comment if he'd talked to her. Maybe he understood that we were fooling around and didn't want the details. He'd been polite but frosty with me since Kelly's graduation binge.

A minute later we pulled up to St. Mark's Catholic

Church in Shoreview. The group out front was pretty small as weddings go, maybe thirty people. Kelly and I joined the crowd. I greeted Angelo's parents, who were even shorter than he was, and then left Kelly with the girls and went to find the guys in the church. Danny was Angelo's best man and was helping out, keeping him cool, making sure he didn't run off to Florida or anything.

As I walked into the conference room in the back of the church, Angelo was in a chair and Thaddeus and Danny were standing behind him, each massaging one shoulder. "He's all tense, Jackson," Thaddeus explained. "His shoulders are like rocks."

"Relax, Angelo," I said. "Nothing to it. Just say, 'I do.'"

"Yeah, easy for you to say, you have so much experience," Angelo smiled. "I'm cool, guys. Really. My body just disagrees."

Danny, Thaddeus, and I began escorting guests into the church a few minutes later. The ceremony was simple and sweet, with a Catholic Mass and traditional vows. Near the end, the priest encouraged anyone wanting to receive Communion to step forward. As best man, Danny was right next to Angelo, and so he just followed along after his friend, even though he wasn't Catholic and didn't really grasp the ritual.

"Body of Christ," the priest said, holding out the wafer. Danny took it in his hand, turned it over for further examination, then shrugged and popped it in his mouth like a breath mint. Giggles and gasps momentarily disrupted the sacrament. The priest frowned and next to me Thaddeus was shaking he was trying so hard not to laugh.

I thought Angelo and Debbie looked good together, about the same size and with matching dark hair and eyes. She didn't look pregnant to me, but I'm no expert.

Kelly thought she saw some subtle signs. "That's going to be a good-looking kid," she whispered when we were in the back of the church waiting for the photographer to set up.

"Well, if you're right, he'll probably be a jock, too. Angelo played basketball and baseball and Debbie was on the cross-country team."

"How do you know their kid will be a boy?"

"Hey, I don't even know if there's going to be a kid, Miss Snoopy. But if there is, I just sort of assumed it'd be a boy. They're both Italian, right, so it's like in *The Godfather*." I tried out a whispered Marlon Brando. "'May your first child be a masculine child.'"

Kelly had to stifle her laughter. Looking at her with her glove half covering her pretty mouth, I felt a surge of joy. I'd never given marriage much thought before meeting her, except to consider why so many people started off loving each other and ended up hating each other, like my folks. But I'd been thinking of marriage more often lately. We called our relationship "serious" when asked, although I wondered sometimes just how serious it was, given that she was heading off to college in a couple of months.

Since I was in church, I decided to talk over the situation with Granny. I'd gotten into the habit of informal prayers, and liked to think of God and people who died in a casual way, like we were still friends or relatives or whatever. Seemed natural, even if it was borderline blasphemy. I just couldn't think of God as Mr. Infinite Power who I should fear because he could send me on a fast break to hell. Likewise, just because people died I couldn't think of them as saints or holy heroes, as Granny put it. I knew she'd be cool with us still talking like always, even if her death put a strain on the conversation.

Kelly and I both liked movies, including older ones like *The Godfather* and that Australian movie, *Crocodile Dundee*. One of my favorite parts of the second one was when Dundee says, "Me and God, we're mates." I had Kelly stop the DVD and replay that scene because it sounded so honest to me.

Anyway, I brought up the marriage topic while we were driving to the reception at the Moose Lodge north of town. Kelly looked at me like I was joking for a second, then her face became a mask of horror.

"Jackson, we've talked about this," she said. "You know I'm going to Princeton. Then I'll be going to graduate school. Then I'll be starting a career. So when exactly am I supposed to get married?"

"Anytime in there would be okay with me," I said. "I love you, Kelly."

The silence that followed spoke pretty loudly. I looked over at her. Her eyes were on the floor, head nodding slightly the way it did when she was deep in thought. "Jackson, let's be fashionably late to the reception. We need to talk, and I don't want to talk in the parking lot of the Moose Lodge while everyone is pulling in. Let's go to that park by Silver Lake."

It was our first make-out spot and just a few minutes away. I parked in the shade of a large oak tree and we rolled down the windows. The setting sun behind us turned the lake gold.

"Let me ramble a bit, without interruption," she said. "First of all, yes, I do love you. You looked so hurt when I didn't reply with the standard cliché, but your statement was more of a challenge than an affectionate summation of your feelings."

I started to protest and she held up her hand.

"Without interruption, please. Now it is obvious that we're not going to be together come September. You don't even have a plan or a goal that far in advance. That bothers me, I must admit. I love being with you, but I think our differences could be major roadblocks in the years ahead." I could tell she'd rehearsed the speech a few times. I wondered if her father had helped write it.

"So I'll tell you what I want, Jackson. I want us to have fun this summer. I want to go sailing with you and hang out at the beach, and just have a blast. Then I want to be a freshman at Princeton. I want us to remain close, and see each other when we can. Who knows, maybe we will get married one day. But I'm not ready to promise anything about that now."

I waited to be sure she was done. I was pretty stunned.

I thought Kelly loved me as much as I loved her, and kind of assumed we'd be together the rest of our lives.

"Well?" she asked.

"Well, I don't know. I need to think."

"Fair enough. Please don't be mad at me. I'm telling you my honest feelings, not trying to hurt you."

"I'm not mad," I said. "Or hurt." At the moment, in my shell-shocked condition, this was true. But I sensed I had the potential to be one pissed off dude in the near future.

We drove over to the reception. We danced and partied, and I drank enough beer to take my mind off what Kelly said. She snuggled close during the slow songs, I held her tight, and everything seemed as wonderful as before. Yet a part of me knew that everything had changed. During one dance I spaced out and thought about working as a bus driver in Princeton so I could be close to her, drive her around sometimes, and win her back…Stupid daydreams. Like she would want me stalking after her at Princeton. Like she would fall for a bus driver.

Near the end of the reception, Danny walked over to our table and sat down between Kelly and I, placing his big arms around our shoulders. He'd long ago abandoned his tux jacket on the back of a chair. The collar of his white shirt was open and his bow tie hung limply. "So how you two lovebirds doing?" he asked, squeezing us together in a group hug. "I'm predicting you two will be the next to get hitched."

Kelly and I looked at each other for a second, then

laughed. She kept on laughing long after I'd stopped, convulsing and almost crying.

"What?" Danny asked. "What'd I say?"

I said, "Your timing is incredible, you know that?"

He stood up and winced. "Oops, trouble in paradise...Come on, Jax, help me and Thaddeus get the bats out of my trunk."

We walked into the warm night. "So you and Kelly have a blowup?" he asked.

"Not really, more a discussion about the future. She has one, I don't. End of story."

"That story sucks," Danny said.

"What's this about you not having a future, Jackson?" Thaddeus asked when we reached the car. Since he'd self-destructed during the basketball season, almost killing himself and doing serious drugs, he'd done a major turnaround. Coach Johns at Penn told him he'd take a chance with a scholarship if Thaddeus went to rehab and counseling, which he did.

Now he was Mr. Super Clean, as Danny put it. He took off last night when we headed to the club. "Coach told me I got to keep three things in mind when socializing," he'd told us. "Time, place, and substance. Right now it's one a.m., you're all going to a strip club, and I'm sure there will be alcohol involved, and drugs available if you ask the right dude. I'm out, guys. See you tomorrow."

Thaddeus was also talking lately about being a drug and alcohol counselor when his playing days were over. I always thought he'd be a great basketball coach, because he's patient, knows the game, and understands how to motivate people...But I guess those traits would serve a counselor pretty well, too.

At the reception, Thaddeus thought I needed motivating. "Look, Jax," he said, "you're a really good ballplayer and high jumper, and smart when you put your mind to it. I'm not lying to you. Your future could be great. You just gotta decide what you're gonna do, set some goals."

"So everyone keeps telling me. You'll know when I know, Thaddeus."

"No, not good enough," he said, shaking his head.

"That's the best I can do."

"Nah, I'm not buying it."

"Me either," Danny added.

"What do you guys want from me?" I asked.

"Well, how about if you set some goals right now?" Thaddeus asked. "Short-term, end-of-summer goals. We'll be your witnesses and stay on your case about getting there."

I blew out a breath, thinking it over. It was cool they cared about me that much. "How about if I have a firm plan in place by August?" I said. "You guys are busy the rest of this month and July, but you gotta come out sailing with me in August. Angelo, too. And I'll give you a progress report."

Danny and Thaddeus looked at each other and nodded. "Don't put it off until the last minute, start implementing your plan as you go," Danny said.

"Right," Thaddeus nodded. "Like if you decide to go

to JC and play ball, you start a tough workout program and focus on that, maybe take a study skills class like I am."

"Okay, agreed," I said, though part of me didn't like the idea of disappointing Conrad, even if he was a jerk at times.

We brought most of the bats inside, then I returned to the parking lot to retrieve mine from the brown beast. Danny came with me.

"When you gonna sell that thing?" he asked.

"Sell the old beast? No way, it was a gift from Granny."

"I doubt she'd mind, Jackson. Especially with all the money you spend on gas."

"Yeah, it does guzzle the stuff…I just haven't thought about selling her."

"You should. Get yourself a little sports car or motor-cycle."

The idea was appealing. "I'll get back to you," I said.

We hauled the bats inside and distributed them after the bouquet tossing. Kelly, I noticed, had to be yanked from her chair by two other girls. The bouquet came toward her, just a bit high; with her height and long arms she could have grabbed it easily, but she let it sail on by. This was the exclamation point of the evening, I thought.

After the girls cleared the floor, a dozen of us guys lined up facing each other, bats in hand. Then we began clanking the bats overhead, forming an arch sort of like the military sword thing. Angelo and Debbie ran between the lines, out of the hall, and into their car, then drove off to their new life together.

"Oh my God!" Kelly laughed when I returned to my seat with my bat. "That's the tackiest thing I've ever seen!"

"Just some harmless fun," I said, although I must admit I thought it was pretty silly when Danny first told me about it.

"I didn't mean it the way it sounded," she said. "Sorry."

We drove through the quiet streets at midnight. I didn't feel like talking, but I didn't want her to think I was pissed and have her explore any more feelings on the subject, either. So I told her about working at the boatyard and Conrad and living aboard a sailboat.

"Looks like everyone's asleep," she said as I pulled up to her darkened house. "You want to come in for a while? We could go down to the rec room in the basement."

I knew what that meant, and I'd always been only too willing to fool around with Kelly. But I heard myself saying, "No, better not. I'm tired, got a long drive back to Manasquan."

Kelly nodded with her head down. I thought she might be waiting for me to kiss her goodnight. If so, it was going to be a long wait. She opened the door a moment later. "Call me after you think things through, Jackson," she said. "And try to see my point of view."

She walked swiftly to her house, heels clicking on the driveway, and I had a terrible feeling that it might be the last time I'd ever see her.

NINE

*"It struck me that he was joyous in a fero-
cious sort of way; that he was glad there was
an impending struggle, that he was thrilled
and upborne with knowledge that one of the
great moments of living, when the tide of life
surges up in a flood, was upon him."*

—Jack London

My watch alarm woke me as usual at six a.m. It took
me a minute to remember that it was Sunday, my
one day off, and I didn't have to be at the boatyard. I knew
I couldn't go back to sleep, so I leaned over to my little
kitchen on the other side of the boat and poured water
from a gallon jug into the tea kettle, put the kettle on the
hot plate burner, and turned the setting to high.

While I waited for the water to boil, I looked out the

starboard windows of *Morning Sun*. The nearest piling had a seagull on top that seemed to be staring at me. When I returned home last night, the tide was out and the piling towered overhead. Conrad was right—I rose and fell with the tides, my body just a couple of feet above the water, and never noticed.

The kettle whistled. I flipped off the burner and deposited a packet of oatmeal into my one bowl, some honey into my one cup, then poured the steaming water over both. I mixed them with my one spoon and put an Irish Breakfast tea bag into the cup to brew while I ate the oatmeal.

Granny had introduced me to tea, which she insisted I drink for breakfast instead of my usual can of soda. I couldn't stand coffee and thought of tea as similar, but of course it was much different. Now I drank a cup of tea every morning, and often thought of Granny telling me not to let the bag sit in the water for more than three minutes or it would turn bitter. "Mind your bag," she'd say.

Leaning back and sipping my tea, I felt satisfied. Lots of people eat breakfast in bed on Sunday morning, but hardly any can make breakfast in bed.

Then of course I remembered Angelo's wedding and the current Kelly situation. And I felt betrayed. I felt like she set me up to fall in love with her, and was now running away and saying, "Just kidding!"

I wouldn't call her. Let her call me, or forget the whole thing…Going to Princeton. Geez, what was I doing with a Princeton girl anyway? There were thousands of hot girls around Manasquan, and I'd noticed some of them checking me out—the sun was having a positive influence on my zits, no doubt about it. I'd work up the nerve to talk to the next one I saw looking my way, see what happened.

After cleaning the dishes, I read an essay on waves in the book Gerry gave me, read a chapter of *The Proving Ground*, about an Australian sailing race gone to hell, reviewed navigation in the sailing manuals, and practiced my knots. Kelly and Granny kept interrupting my reading. I'd find myself thinking of them and not comprehending the words, mad at one and missing the other. I had to go back and read the passages again, straining to focus. I didn't finish until almost ten.

I pulled the hatch and looked around. Overcast, with a strong wind from the east. I had to do something to take my mind off Kelly, and I had a couple of ideas. First, I called Danny.

"Yeah," he said in a groggy voice.

"You're not up yet?"

"Jackson, I'm hungover and won't be up until noon at the earliest. Go back to bed, dude."

"No, I'm going sailing. Why don't you help me buy a new used vehicle later this afternoon?"

"Okay, cool. Call me back after one. You got that? After one."

He hung up before I could promise to let him recover in peace. I put on my swim trunks, a T-shirt, sunglasses, and sailing hat. I grabbed my running shoes and tossed them into the cockpit of the *Sunfish*, which I kept on the port side of *Morning Sun*. The slip was made for two boats in the twenty-three- to twenty-six-foot range. I slipped the *Sunfish* between the two larger boats. Pretty snug, and the owner of the other boat might have objected if he was ever around, because no matter how well I tied down the *Sunfish*, she banged around a little during storms.

It didn't adversely affect the other sailboat, a twenty-three-foot Coronado named *Miss Ann* that was covered with green slime and a ratty blue sail cover on the boom. Grass was growing in a couple of fertile spots, and it looked like no one had cleaned her in five years. I thought about washing her off a few times, to be a nice neighbor, but it was just too gross and too far gone. The few times I sprayed *Miss Ann* with the hose when I was cleaning *Morning Sun*, sort of as a test, the slime seemed to eat the water. It would take me a whole day just to get her into the pretty damn bad category.

Forget about it.

On *Morning Sun*, I went forward and grabbed the tiller and centerboard from my V-berth, closed the hatch, and stepped down gently onto the *Sunfish*. She rocked a bit, then settled down while I snapped in the tiller and unwound the lines from around the sail.

In five minutes, I was ready to cruise. I released the dock lines and backed her out by pushing off on *Morning Sun* on one side and *Miss Ann* on the other. Dipping my right hand into the comparatively clean marina water to wash it off, I thought the owner should rename *Miss Ann* something like *Disgusting* or *Miss Crud*.

I was anxious to get the day rolling and pushed myself blindly and swiftly into the dock lane. I'd forgotten Conrad's advice about checking all directions and moving the boat slowly around the marina. "Boats," he'd told me many times, "don't come with brakes."

Fortunately, there was no traffic in my part of the marina. Not much elsewhere, either. Most boaters didn't start showing up until around noon on Sundays. And maybe the wind was too much for most of them.

Not for me. I dropped the centerboard and gave the tiller a few yanks to get the bow pointed toward the harbor, then raised the sail. I was prepared this time, leaning over the side as I pulled the halyard. My weight compensated for the sudden gust of wind that caught the red and white sail. I tied off the halyard—the cleat knot was almost automatic now—and picked up the sheet with my right hand. I scooted back to the cockpit and pushed the tiller hard with my left hand; the sudden gust had the boat heading toward a powerboat on the opposite dock.

Now I could relax a bit. I angled toward the wind near the end of the dock, so I could head upwind and stop the boat if any traffic was on a collision course in the river harbor. It was all clear, so I pulled the tiller toward me and hauled in the sheet, and began tacking back and forth across the river in the general direction of the ocean a quarter-mile away.

It was blowing harder out at sea; it looked a little scary,

with lots of whitecaps on the gray-green water, spray around the jetties from the breaking waves, and rollers coming far up the river. What the heck, I thought. This is how you learn. I noticed my running shoes in the cockpit and tied them to the mast. The *Sunfish* flipped pretty easily—I'd gone over a half-dozen times since I started sailing her—and I didn't want to lose my shoes to the ocean floor.

Once I cleared the jetty, I pulled in the sheet tight and came about, ducking under the boom as it swept past and crossing to the port side. The *Sunfish* almost went over as she turned south, but I leaned back and let the sail out and she recovered. The wind was so strong I had to leave the sail far out to stay under control. One of the key sailing arts, I found, was how far to let the sail in or out. When the wind was coming from the side on a beam reach, you sailed best when you hauled the sail in tight—but if you hauled too tight a gust sent you right into the water. Let it out too much and the boat moved sluggishly. With some practice, I'd developed a decent feel for the wind.

This was the fastest I'd moved in a sailboat, and it was a thrill, like running a fast break and soaring for a dunk. I was skimming along the waves for the most part, but every now and then I'd hit one wrong and the bow would rise out of the water and slam down hard. I was soaked in less than a minute.

I looked around and was surprised no other boats were out. It felt lonely. Still, I was having fun, and was too busy with the sail and tiller to think about Kelly or Granny.

After a couple of miles I picked a spot on the Point Pleasant beach. I let the sail out farther and pulled the tiller toward me, running with the waves.

Next I let down the sail and had to struggle to keep it out of the water. Just when I had that squared away, the *Sunfish* caught a wave and I surfed down a powerful hill of foam. The boat was close to the beach when the wave broke, and I got the centerboard up just in time—I felt it scrape sand for a fraction of a second. Hopping into the foamy water, I guided the boat onto the beach, then went forward and pulled her by the bow handle until she was fifty feet clear of the water.

My shoes were soaked. They squished when I took my first steps, running south on the nearly deserted beach. The wind was stronger here, with gusts pushing me off balance now and then. Although it was a warm breeze, I was wet, and was starting to feel chilled despite the exercise.

I hadn't been working out much, although laboring on boats all day kept me in fair shape. I'd found a middle school playground near the marina and tried to go over to shoot a few hundred jumpers after work every day. Some days I was just too wiped out, though, and just relaxed on *Morning Sun.* I'd shoot imaginary jumpers, read my sailing books, and crash, feeling slightly guilty.

I enjoyed the run, despite the heavy winds. I ran a mile or so, then turned back. I was planning to take a swim as well, but it was too rough—the wind seemed to be picking up even more, and I knew it would be another workout getting back to my slip.

After retying my shoes to the mast, I turned the *Sunfish* around and pulled her back into the ocean. When she was deep enough, I put down the centerboard. The *Sunfish* glided through the first few waves, but when I was chest deep my timing was off, and the next wave almost flipped her. Only my weight in front kept her from going over. As it was I wrenched my arm and the wave took us in about twenty feet.

The next attempt I stayed in the stern and shoved her through the big waves before they curled and crashed. It worked, but on the last one I ended up far behind the *Sunfish* and had to swim to catch up. I managed to awkwardly climb aboard in the rough water. The boat spun north naturally, so I just had to raise the sail—and when I did we were flying again.

"Yeeeeeee-haaaaawwwww!" I yelled into the wind. The conditions made it both frightening and exhilarating, and I cruised along on the razor edge of control. A few times I ended up sitting on the underside of the boat, leaning back as far as I could, with the sail almost touching the water—but she stayed upright. My heart was beating fast and I knew that if the wind was slightly stronger I'd be in trouble; the sail just couldn't take much more wind and the boat would capsize, over and over again, every time I tried to sail.

A hard rain began to pelt me in the back. It turned the world gray, but I could make out the dark rocks of the south jetty. I had to steer toward the wind to clear the jetty, and I realized too late that I should have been taking the *Sunfish* on a northeast course all along. By heading slightly toward the wind, I would have had better control of the boat and a better angle of approach to the river.

The problem was that toward the wind in this case was also toward the open ocean, and it was looking evil out there. Black clouds hovered on the horizon and I saw a couple of lightning strikes. I just wanted to be back at the marina now, safe and warm, sipping hot chocolate on *Morning Sun*.

As I cleared the jetty, I pulled the tiller toward me and let out the sail slightly for the run upriver. But the boat was heading north too fast, and a large wave increased her speed, and I saw that she was going to hit the rocks on the north jetty.

I had a moment of absolute panic in which I froze. I suppose that's how it would be if someone suddenly pointed a gun at you from close range. Recovering, I let go of the sheet and leaned forward onto the bow. I grabbed the mast pole with my left hand and pushed myself farther forward on the bow, until I could reach the handle with the tip with my right hand. Only my long arms enabled me to do this without going overboard.

My legs hung over the side of the *Sunfish*. Holding the mast with my left hand and the bow handle with my right, I felt like I was Jesus on the cross. Forgetting my previous declaration of friendship with God, I was pleading with the Almighty Father and Glorious Savior to get me out of this mess. I wondered whether my crucifixion posture hurt or helped my case.

A boulder was coming up fast and I kicked out with my right leg and pushed off on it before it hit the hull. I continued pushing off rocks like this as the waves took the boat up the river.

About the seventh time I pushed off the rocks, I gave the *Sunfish* enough distance to recover. Staying low, I slid toward the stern, hooked my feet into the cockpit, then pulled the rest of my body. I straightened the tiller and hauled in the sheet, which had gone out as far as the line allowed. A knot at the end kept it from dangling in the water. The *Sunfish* stayed clear of the rocks by a couple of feet and I turned her southeast toward the middle of the river. I was sailing again and the boat was under control. My heart took a minute to stop booming.

As I cruised up the river, relieved and exhausted, I saw Conrad standing with some sailors aboard the Coast Guard cutter moored outside the marina. They were all staring at me. I was too tired to be embarrassed, so I just gave them a little smile and wave. One of the younger sailors waved back; the others just stared daggers.

"Come aboard and talk to us after you get tied up," an officer shouted. I nodded and shouted okay. Conrad just shook his head.

My legs were vibrating as I stood on the dock and tied up the *Sunfish*. "Thanks for getting me back here," I said, patting her hull. I thanked God, too, since it was a team effort. On *Morning Sun* I gathered some dry clothes, a towel, sneakers, and my raincoat and put them in my backpack. I went up to the marina bathrooms. A hot shower cost a quarter for three minutes, and so I'd learned to be efficient. This time, though, I spent a dollar and got warm and clean. My right foot had a few cuts from the rocks and I washed it clean and applied some disinfectant and Band-Aids.

The storm had grown worse; I had to lean into the wind and rain as I walked over to meet with the Coast Guard. I asked for permission to come aboard and they waved me into the cabin. I accepted the tea they offered, along with a lecture about checking weather reports and small craft advisory warnings before heading out to sail.

"You're dumb, lucky, or brave, maybe all three," the officer concluded. "You need to listen more carefully to Mr. Dean. He'll tell you all you need to know about sailing." The respect in his voice made it clear that Conrad had earned his reputation as a tough old salt. I looked over at him, expecting him to launch into another obscenity-heavy list of my shortcomings as a human being in general and sailor in particular.

"Interesting maneuver along the jetty," he said. "Don't think they teach that one in the sailing schools. Saved my boat, anyhow." They all chuckled and smiled at me, and despite the mistakes I had the feeling I at least did something right.

TEN

*"Holding course by swells seems always to be
a matter more of feel than sight."*

—David Lewis

Because of the storm, Danny and I rescheduled our
vehicle search for later in the week. I worked my
butt off at the yard, which helped me take my mind off
Kelly and Granny during the day. Of course they invaded
my thoughts when I was reading in my bunk or walking around the marina at night. When my phone rang
Wednesday night, I was hoping it was Kelly, even though I
was still mad at her.

"Hello?"

"Hey there, Jackson," the familiar voice said. "This is your father."

I was surprised and speechless for a couple of seconds; we hadn't talked in over a year, although we'd been writing to each other the last few months. "Hi," I said finally. "How's it going?"

"Very well. Wonderful, in fact. I just won a big case. It was my first with this firm, so I'm suddenly the fair-haired boy." He sounded excited and proud, and I could hear a party going on around him. I remembered that it was a few hours earlier in Los Angeles.

"Congratulations," I said. "Must have been a big case." Part of me, I must admit, was wondering how much he was celebrating.

"Thanks, it was. It's kind of noisy in here right now, an impromptu party broke out…But don't you worry, I'm only drinking sparkling cider."

"Good. That's good."

"I've learned my lesson," he added. "Never again…Anyway, I wanted to apologize for not making your graduation."

"No big deal," I said. "I know you were working this new job and everything."

"Still and all, I wish I could have made it out there… You know I am going to be at our New York office for a couple of days in mid-August, and I was thinking of taking a week's vacation…it would be great to see you and Shannon."

"Sure," I said. "I'm living and working down in Manasquan."

"I heard, I heard. How is that going, son?"

I didn't like the "son" bit. Yeah, I was his son, but it felt like he was forcing the father thing on me, and it was too late for that. "It's going fine, Jack," I said. I didn't want him to feel bad, just remember that his former father role was gratefully gone, and we were in the early stages of a new friendship. He caught the emphasis and called me by name the rest of the conversation, which went pretty well.

I told him about the boatyard and learning to sail, including my recent misadventure. Before he went back to the party, I knew I had to clear one thing up. "It'll be good to see you," I said. "But I have to tell you, I'm not sure about Shannon and Mom."

"I know," he said quietly. "I'm hoping for the best. I'll have to wait and see."

"Okay. Thanks for calling. And congratulations again."

"It was good to hear your voice, Jackson."

．　．　．

Danny was sprawled on the hood of his exquisitely maintained Ford Tempo when I pulled into his driveway the following evening. He was wearing cutoff shorts and a red sleeveless T-shirt that showed off his muscular guns. "Better get off your car before you dent the hood and flatten the tires," I joked.

"Muscle car can handle a muscle guy," he shot back.

Calling a Ford Tempo a muscle car was a stretch of the imagination, but I knew he was proud of his wheels so I let it go.

He slid off the front of the car and grabbed his basketball out of the backseat, just to hold while we talked. He was going through the same transition away from the game as I was, more or less. He'd never practiced as much as I did and he played other sports, but basketball was his number one. I knew he just liked the feel of the ball in his hands. He passed it over to me after a few minutes.

"So what are you going to replace the beast with?" he asked.

"You're not going to believe it," I said, throwing the ball back to him. "I'm getting a motorcycle."

"Tight, that's tight, Jax. Gotta say, though, you're not a motorcycle guy in the classic sense."

"What do you mean?"

"I mean my mom drives faster than you," he said. "You drive like a senior citizen with a baby on board. Face it, you're slow, and well, I associate motorcycles with speed."

What he said annoyed me, probably because it was true. I didn't think of myself as a slow driver—it's just that Danny, Thaddeus, and Angelo were all speed demons, and I'd feel bad if I ever damaged Granny's beast. I'd argued responsibility and my relative speed theory before, without convincing them.

"There's no law that says you have to drive a motorcycle

fast," I argued now. "But I'll drive it faster than I do the beast."

"Promises, promises. Listen, I know a guy who has a lot on the southeast side of town, sells used cars, trucks, motorcycles, everything. Why don't we hit there first?"

"Sounds good," I said. Following Danny over to the used car lot, I lost him within a half-mile. I was trying to keep up, to prove I was a fast driver when I felt like it, but he had the better car. Plus, he accelerated through turns and I hadn't mastered that technique. I had a rough idea where the lot was; he also told me it was called Gorilla Cars and I should look for the gorilla on a swing if I lost him.

I continued to the southeast side, and a mile later spotted Danny's car idling on the side of the road. He smiled in the rearview mirror and cut me off as he peeled away from the curb.

He parked way down the street from the lot. I could see the gorilla sitting in a swing that dangled atop the dealership's roof. "Why are we parking out here?" I asked.

"We're not," he said, leaning against his car. "We'll pull into the lot in a minute. I just wanted to talk strategy first."

"Strategy? For buying a used motorcycle?"

"You need a strategy for every transaction," he explained, sounding like the lawyer he planned to become after college. It was always kind of funny hearing his formal-talk voice come out of that tough-guy face. "Otherwise, Jax," he continued, "you get lousy deals. People take advantage of the weak and unsuspecting. That's the way the world is."

"Makes sense," I agreed, never really having thought of it that way. "But I don't know anything about motorcycles and how much they should cost."

"I know a little," he said. "But knowledge isn't as important as strategy. What's the most you're willing to spend?"

I'd saved the money Granny left me, along with the graduation gifts, and added some more from my checks at the boatyard. I had almost three grand in the bank, and didn't want to lose too much. "I was hoping for a straight-up trade," I said. "I really don't want to spend more than a thousand."

"No way you're going to get a straight-up trade," he said. "Anybody can see the beast is on her last legs, and car salesmen have to make some money on the deal. We'll keep a thousand as our final offer…And Jackson, I do the dealing, agreed?"

"I guess," I shrugged. "You probably need the negotiating practice for your future career."

"More important, my old man is a fantastic salesman, and I've gone with him every time we bought and sold a car. I know the tricks of the trade. So why don't you watch and learn this time?"

"Yes, boss," I said sarcastically.

"And don't miss your cue when I give it to you," he said, moving toward his car.

"What cue?" I asked, but he ignored me and drove off.

The sun was setting when we parked at Gorilla Cars.

A chunky, gray-haired salesman in a sky blue sports jacket stamped out his cigarette and moved toward us with a smile.

"Young Danny Larson," he said, shaking hands. "Where's your old man?"

"Just me today, John," he said. "Me and my friend Jackson here."

He shook hands and smiled, mentioned the weather, got me talking about boats somehow, and told us a semi-related fishing story before Danny cut him off.

"What do you have in the way of motorcycles?" he asked.

"Some nice ones. Follow me over this way," he said, leading us past the trucks toward the back of the lot. "What are you looking to get for the Ford?"

"Ford's not for sale," Danny said. "The station wagon is."

John stopped and gave us an appraising look. "That's your car, Jackson?"

"Yeah."

"I see. Well, how much are you looking for?"

"He's looking for a straight-up trade, car for bike," Danny said.

John kept smiling when he said, "I thought I was dealing with Jackson, Danny boy?"

"I'm negotiating for him."

"Oh, I get it. His attorney to be named later."

"Something like that."

"Jackson here looks old enough to deal for himself,"

he said with a wink. I immediately felt defensive. Then I realized that's exactly what he wanted me to feel.

"I negotiate boat deals," I said. "I let Danny handle my car business."

We all laughed and he took us to the motorcycles. He went through various features, discussing the chassis design and steering geometry and other technical aspects.

"Which is the best bike?" Danny asked.

"Hard to say. Personally, I'd go for the Honda."

"You'd personally go for it, or it's the one you're trying to get rid of?"

The big smile again. "Got me, Danny. I should know better when I'm dealing with a Larson. The Suzuki Intruder 800 is the best bike on the lot. No lie. It's four years old, in great shape."

"How much?"

"How much you got?"

"Nothing," Danny shrugged. "We want a straight-up trade."

"Forget it, boys. I don't need another piece-of-crap car," he said. "No offense, Jackson."

"Well, we'll give you the car—which is also in excellent condition, by the way—and $400 if we like the way she handles."

They haggled some more, exchanging good-natured insults, while I looked over the red and black motorcycle. John walked over and put his hand on my shoulder. "Let me get the key," he said. "You take her for a spin, Jackson, while Danny and I talk business."

Once again I felt like a kid he'd thrown a lollipop, a little bribe to keep him quiet while the adults talked. When he was out of earshot I said, "Hey Danny, what's my cue supposed to be?"

"You'll know it when you hear it," he said in a whisper.

I'd never been on a motorcycle before. John asked if I'd driven a car with a stick shift, I said yes, and he explained that the concept was pretty much the same. I had a couple of false starts, then got the hang of it. I drove the cycle around the block three times, and felt more comfortable each time. She did handle well.

When I got back to the lot, I dismounted and said, "I'll take her."

Danny's mouth dropped open. He threw up his hands in disgust. "Allow me to consult with my client," he said. John smiled some more and held up his own hands in innocence.

Danny grabbed me in a headlock and led me swiftly over to the trucks. "Hey, dude, that hurts!"

"What the hell are you doing?" he said, shoving me away. He was really angry.

"What? I like it. I want to buy it."

"You want to pay through the nose for it, too?"

"No…Like we said, a thousand tops."

"I was working the deal," he said, pacing in circles, "talking him down, and here you come, announcing you'll take it. Jesus, Jackson, why don't you just throw your money into the ocean?"

"Okay, okay, sorry."

"We got one last chance here," he said. "I have to give you the cue sooner than expected because you opened your big mouth. Be ready."

We walked back over to John, who was leaning on the bike. "You've made a fine choice, Jackson," he said. "I'll take that old heap and give this beautiful bike to you for fourteen-hundred."

"Thanks, John," Danny said, "but we decided to look around some more." I was looking at the gleaming bike, and it took me a second to realize that he'd just given me the cue.

"Yeah," I said quickly. "That's a nice bike, but we want to check some other dealers over in Highland. I have a friend with a Honda for sale." Lying seemed to come naturally on the used car lot, and no one took offense.

"You aren't going to get a better deal," he said.

Danny went and shook hands. "We'll see. Thanks again. Take it easy."

I began walking off with him. When we got to his car, he whispered, "If he lets us drive away, then you know fourteen hundred is the best deal he's willing to offer. If he stops us, we know there's room to negotiate."

I nodded and continued across the lot. John came running up after Danny started his car and I was opening the door of the beast. "Tell you what, Jackson. You seem like a nice young guy, and I know you liked that bike. Twelve-fifty and she's yours."

"I really can't spend more than eight hundred," I said as Danny walked over. He heard me and gave me the OK sign behind the salesman's back. "Can't do eight hundred, no sir, no way," John said, shaking his head. He and Danny took up the negotiations again, and after a half-hour they settled on a thousand, helmet included. They parted with smiles and handshakes. I wrote the check, filled out the paperwork, patted the beast goodbye, and followed Danny back to his house aboard my new ride.

"Pizza's on me tonight," I said as I removed the helmet. "You got me a good deal."

"Well, at least you picked up the cue," he said, slapping my shoulder hard. "But Jax, after just saving you four-hundred bucks, the pizza is on you for the rest of the summer, buddy."

We negotiated that point while we shot around and waited for the deliveryman.

ELEVEN

"Meditation and water are wedded for ever."

—Herman Melville

The next Sunday, after a relaxing morning sail on the *Sunfish*, I was taking a siesta aboard *Morning Sun* when I heard a splash. I figured it was just a fish jumping or something; I'd seen a few come several feet out of the water with a harbor seal in hot pursuit. I put my arm back over my eyes, then heard another splash. Pretty unlikely coincidence. I stood and pulled back the hatch and looked around. Concentric circles were spreading in the water about five feet behind the boat.

I heard a whistle and turned to see Gerry standing outside the marina gate, holding a rock. "Let me in," he yelled through cupped hands, "or I may take down your ship with the next toss."

"Hold on a sec," I yelled back. I'd been lounging in just my underwear, so I threw on some shorts, a T-shirt, and sandals and was ready to go in twenty seconds. The boating life had its advantages.

"How you been?" I asked as I strode up the ramp to the gate. I hadn't seen him since graduation.

"Wonderful," he said with a smile. I noticed he was still as skinny as when he'd returned from Europe. His bicycle was leaning against the fence.

"You should have called and let me know you were coming," I said as I pushed open the gate. "I would have been looking for you."

He followed me down the ramp with his left hand guiding the bicycle by the seat. "No problem, Jax, it was more or less an impromptu trip. I needed a good ride. Downhill most of the way here, so I'll get my workout on the way back."

"Twenty miles uphill," I noted. "You'll get a great workout."

We put his bicycle in the cockpit of *Morning Sun*. Gerry suggested lunch and I told him I was just getting hungry myself. We walked up to Duggan's at the marina.

We ordered pitchers of water and lemonade, along with a fish burger for me and salad for him.

"This biking is as tough as running track," he said as he finished his first glass of water. "I sort of assumed that since you're sitting on your butt, it wouldn't be so tough. It is once you start putting some serious mileage behind you."

"You're really getting into it."

"Yeah, I haven't used my car once since Granny's funeral. I'm in pretty fair shape."

"You going to race?"

"No, to be honest, I seem to have lost my competitive instinct," he said.

I stared at him for a moment, to see if he was joking. He wasn't. "Hey, I thought you were kidding. You were pretty competitive as a golf coach and in our hoops games in the driveway not so long ago."

He smiled and shook his head. "You're right. Hate to admit it, but you're right."

"Well, as much as you're riding the bike, you should enter a race for fun, just to see how you do."

"Yeah, maybe I'll do that down the line," he said. "In the meantime I'm planning to tour long distances. I have a trip planned out from here to Colorado in late August and early September."

"Seriously?"

"Yeah, be a great way to see the country. I figure if I ride a hundred miles a day, I could get to Boulder, Colorado, in about three weeks."

"Wow, that's a trip. You'll have to show me pictures when you get back."

"That I will. How about you? Planning any big sailing excursions?"

"No, I'm still in the learning phase. I'm going to start taking the bigger boat out soon, maybe for a weekend trip later. After that, I don't know."

"Glad you seem to be enjoying the life," he said. "I almost felt guilty arranging things with Conrad and all."

"Yeah, he can be a pain sometimes, riding me to get work done, yelling if it's not perfect. We almost got into a fist fight the first time we sailed together. And then some days we get along fine and I kind of like the old guy."

"Granny mentioned Conrad to me over the years. She said he was more bark than bite. He's had it rough since the accident."

My fish burger was halfway to my mouth, but I stopped to ask the obvious question.

"He hasn't told you?" Gerry asked.

"No. What happened?"

He sat silently and stared toward the marina. It was like he'd fallen into a trance. I munched my burger and waited for him to snap out of it.

"Sorry, Jax," he said at last. "I thought he'd have told you by now. I can't say more because I heard it in confidence."

"Ah, come on, you can't leave me hanging!"

"Hate to, but no choice. I'm sure he'll tell you eventually. The details aren't important. Just understand that he's had a rough life and be compassionate with him, even when he's not the same with you."

"Yeah, okay." I didn't want to push him any harder because I could tell he felt uncomfortable with the subject. My curiosity would just have to burn.

We talked more about his bike trip and my life at the marina, the motorcycle. Then I asked if he'd decided where to go to graduate school in the fall.

"Yup, I'm enrolled in Naropa University in Colorado. That's where I'm headed on my bike trip."

Again my fish didn't make it to my mouth. "Naropa University? Never heard of it. I mean, that's great, but you could get into Ivy League schools and stuff, or go back to Rutgers...What do your parents think about this?"

"They think I'm crazy," he smiled. "I haven't talked to them since the day after the funeral. I made it clear that I didn't like the way they treated you, which got them angry, and then they really lost it when I told them about my graduate school plans."

"What are you going to study at Naropa?"

"Buddhism, transcendentalism, and Irish literature," he said. "I'm interested in how Buddhist philosophy intersects with the American transcendentalism of Emerson and Thoreau and the Epiphany concept of James Joyce."

"You lost me, buddy. I've heard of epiphany in church and all, and sort of remember Emerson's essay on self-reliance from your class. Kind of vague on the concepts, though."

"Well, to James Joyce an epiphany was a moment of insight that brought pleasure. The 'aha!' phenomenon, if you will. And Emerson and Thoreau were both interested in the beauty of the moment. Both concepts are similar to the Buddhist ideas of an enlightened life. While the traditional Buddhist path to enlightenment is through ever-deeper meditation and ethical living, there have always been some who reach enlightenment without years of effort. They suddenly understood the nature of reality. Sometimes it was an exposure to beauty that did it, sometimes deep pain. In any case, they suddenly understood things with a kind of intuitive grace."

"Whoa, pretty heavy," I said, nibbling on my fries. "And if that's what you're going to study, you'll never get a job."

"Right now I'm not too worried about a job or career," he said. "I'm just taking it a day at a time—actually a moment at a time."

"I was just kidding," I said. "You could always teach and coach."

That made him smile. "A Buddhist basketball coach," he said, nodding his head. "I like it. 'Okay, guys, I don't want you to kick their asses, I want you to get out there and be compassionate!'"

I laughed. "Right, and some parents would probably get upset if you told their kids to win one for the Buddha."

We both laughed for a while. "So if you don't mind

me asking," I said, "what happened to the ambitious, competitive, regular guy teacher I used to know?"

He shrugged. "I changed in my travels. I seemed to walk ambition and competitiveness out of my system."

"What's wrong with ambition and competitiveness?" I asked. The words naturally brought to mind Kelly, who had a lot of both. And being a jock all my life, I always just assumed they were wonderful traits.

"They're overemphasized, in my opinion," he said as he finished his salad and wiped his mouth. "On the one hand, people with those traits are full of life energy, which is fine. On the other hand, they get caught up in future dreams, often at the expense of the present reality. Not to mention present people."

"Yeah, I see your point."

"I've been thinking about it some the last few months. I'm trying to do away with trying, and my only ambition is to grow spiritually. I want it to happen naturally, though, the way a tree grows. The tree doesn't set a five-year goal to be fifty feet tall—it just grows."

I pushed my glass of water over to him. "Here's some nourishment for the tree," I joked. "Seriously, though, I'm surprised you found religion. Granny always worried because you stopped going to church."

"Religion isn't necessarily spiritual. In fact, the rules and rituals can often hinder spiritual growth."

"You know, you're sounding pretty far out there, dude.

I think they're gonna kick us out of here if you start chanting and burning incense."

He smiled and shrugged. "More rituals. But you can see the direction I'm heading."

"Guess you're a Buddhist now."

"Yeah, I started reading about it by chance when I was traveling around Europe. I talked to a few Buddhist monks, listened to lectures. And it inspired me to become a vegetarian and begin meditating…and I converted."

It took me a moment to digest all of this. My fellow Catholic jock friend and former teacher was now a practicing Buddhist. I tried to keep things light while I adjusted to the idea. "So when you're chanting," I asked, "do you say 'OM' or something like that? If I became a vegetarian and meditated, I know I'd think about steak and bacon all the time. Instead of 'OM,' I'd say 'YUM.'"

"I must admit that stuff smelled good to me for a couple of months," he said. "Now it just doesn't interest me at all. Funny how the mind works." He paused and added, "You know, Jackson, you meditate all the time whether you know it or not. Everyone does. A meditation is anything you think about. I don't actually chant myself—I just watch my thoughts until they disappear."

"Then what?"

"Then nothing. That's the point. Nothingness. Stillness. The simple peace of being. I'm sure you've felt that way sometimes living down here at the ocean."

I remembered times I'd sat in the cockpit of *Morn-*

ing Sun, looking at the stars, or listening to the waves, or watching the gulls glide along. Lately, though, I'd been mostly doing a Kelly and Granny meditation, and it wasn't exactly peaceful.

"Nature enhances the spiritual experience," he continued. "At least it works that way for me."

"Yeah, I've had that peaceful feeling sometimes," I said. "I think I know what you're talking about."

"I'll tell you, I started feeling so much more at ease about everything the more I meditated," he said. "I spent ten days in a Buddhist monastery in France, doing almost nothing but meditating."

"No offense, but that sounds pretty boring."

"See you're getting direct hanging out with Conrad," he winked. "Truth is, I was bored a few times the first few days. Then I adjusted."

"So what else did you do in Europe?"

"Changing the subject?"

"Yeah, before you start levitating and speaking in tongues and stuff."

He laughed. "Guess I am a little preachy about it. Tends to happen to recent converts of any religion. And to answer your question, I took trains from city to city, checked out museums, cathedrals, and the local scene. I stayed at hostels and campgrounds to save money."

"Check out the women, too?"

"Yes. One Italian beauty was especially distracting to my spiritual pursuits."

"What was your favorite city? Rome? Paris?"

"They were wonderful, but I really enjoyed Geneva, Switzerland."

"Up in the Alps?"

"Near them. A couple days later I took a train to Chamonix, a ski town way up in the Alps."

"So what did you like about Geneva?"

"Maybe it was more the experience I had there than the town. I arrived in the evening and checked into a hostel. The next morning I put my heavy pack in a storage locker and went for a croissant and a cup of coffee, thinking about what I wanted to do that day. It's nice when you don't have to do anything."

He was smiling and seemed far away. "So what else happened?"

"Not much," he shrugged. "I decided to take a walk along Lake Geneva. It was gorgeous out, sixty-five degrees and sunny. The Alps were arrayed like angels on the far side of this lake, and I was just rambling along, admiring the view, feeling happy. I went about five or six miles like that and came to a bench in a small park. I sat down to rest for a few minutes before heading back into town…and then I had what Zen Buddhists call a satori, a moment of clarity and peace."

"Sounds like a martial arts kick or something. 'Then I hit him with a satori and down he went.'"

"Glad my spiritual experiences amuse you, Jackson."

"Sorry."

"No, I'm kidding. You keep me from taking myself too seriously."

"So how long did the satori thing last?"

"I'm not sure, exactly. I had no sense of time. It felt like I melted into the lake, the birds, the sky, the old couple nearby, the kids chasing a dog...It almost felt like I was floating above the bench. Just pure peace and joy for a while, maybe a few minutes, maybe an hour or two."

"Wow...You know what it sounds like? Don't laugh, but it sounds like the zone. I mean, I know it was more than that, but I remember the times in games I was playing so well, so naturally, it was sort of like I was watching myself do great things rather than acting myself. A floating kind of feeling, no worries, you know? Same thing when I was clearing the bar in the high jump. Just floating up there for a while. Is that what you mean?"

He nodded. "Yes, that's very close. Have you had any experiences like that sailing?"

"Not exactly, but I've been pretty blissed out on the water sometimes, especially when Conrad isn't around to ruin the mood by yelling at me...Sure you can't tell me what happened to contribute to his surliness?"

"No. But like I said, he'll probably tell you himself eventually."

We walked back to *Morning Sun* after lunch. "By the way," he said as he lowered his bike onto the finger pier. "I got a call from Kelly. I don't want to get into your business, pal, but she's pretty upset about you not calling her. She thinks you just shut her out of your life forever."

I was tempted to explain that I was just mad at her, with good reason.

"I mentioned that she could call you," he added, "but her pride is hurt. Maybe yours is, too. But Jax, pride is a lousy reason to lose a girl like Kelly."

I nodded. "Guess I'd be pretty dumb if I didn't listen to a Buddhist on a bicycle."

"That's right," he laughed as he pushed his bike along the pier. "Most people have to climb a mountain to find a guru like me."

"And what's your advice, wise ten-speed teacher?"

"Three words," he yelled back. "Call the girl!"

TWELVE

"For whatever we lose (like a you or a me) it's always ourselves we find in the sea."

—e. e. cummings

For an hour I sat in the cabin of *Morning Sun* and thought about what I'd say to Kelly. I picked up the phone, put it down. Got up from the bunk, sat back down. I would have paced if there was enough room.

Finally I called her. Naturally, Mr. Armstead answered. He was formally polite, as usual, although he sighed a couple of times. I could almost hear him thinking, *Not the*

O'Connell kid again. Thought that boatyard bastard was out of the picture.

He handed the phone over to Kelly. "Hello?" she said tentatively.

"Hi, Kels, Jackson. How you doing?"

"Hmmm. Fair to partly cloudy. You boating types like weather reports, right?"

"And you Ivy League types like witty conversation," I said, "but I don't think I have much at the moment."

"Don't worry, neither do I. Look, Jackson, I miss you and feel rotten that I hurt you. I was going to call you, but I was a little mad because I don't think you had sufficient empathy for me."

"My empathy was insufficient," I agreed. "I also needed to think things through. I just had lunch with Gerry…"

"Did he tell you I called him?"

"Yeah, he did, but I was probably going to call you anyway, Kelly. You know Gerry. He just gave me a little push."

"I told him not to tell you, then I told him if he wanted to tell you he could," she said. "Deep down I wanted him to tell you."

"He did. We had an interesting conversation. Did you know he's going to ride his bike to Colorado and go to graduate school out there in the fall?"

"Gerry's a wild man."

"He's also really into meditation and Buddhism," I added. "He said we're always meditating about something, and the truth is I've been meditating about you since the wedding. Hours and hours of Kelly meditation."

"That's good to know," she said. "I'm starting to feel the sun break through the clouds. Yes, it's definitely clearing up."

"Good. Want to go for a motorcycle ride?"

"I take this to mean you sold the brown beast. Sure, come on over. I want to see the look on my dad's face when you pull up to the house."

I kept the Intruder in a storage locker I rented, along with my basketball, winter clothes, and books. I was getting a good feel for her on the highway, and trying to be very careful. It helped that—okay, I'll admit it—I'm a pretty slow driver. I'd noticed already that drivers had a harder time seeing motorcycles; a few started pulling their cars into a lane I was occupying. I tried to stay clear of blind spots and be very aware of the vehicles around me, which made the experience more intense than driving a car.

It was getting toward dinnertime by the time I reached the Armstead's. I was hoping Kelly wouldn't invite me inside for another uncomfortable meal. Mr. Armstead, hands on hips and a scowl on his face, watched me pull into his driveway on my bike. He started to say something when Kelly kissed him on the cheek and ran over to me. I turned the bike around, handed her the helmet, and she hopped aboard. We were out of there before he could object.

Kelly snuggled close to me and rested her head on my upper back while linking her hands around my stomach. I was even more careful now that a passenger I loved was aboard and wearing the only helmet. I'd have to buy another.

We headed to an inexpensive restaurant over in Shoreline where we'd had one of our first dates. "Nostalgia time," she said after I parked, turned off the engine, and enjoyed a lingering kiss.

"Not really," I shrugged. "I was just trying to think of a relatively close spot where your father couldn't track us down."

"Well, I believe I'll hear about this until it's time to leave for school." College again. I could tell she hadn't meant to bring it up, but now it hung between us like a mainsail, obstructing communication and threatening to knock us over with a violent jibe.

I waited until we were seated in a booth to get down to business. "Look, Kelly, I want you to go to Princeton, graduate school, all of that. I want to be part of your life, too. So I'm trying to figure out how we can pull it off."

"I want to be part of your life, too. I just don't think we ought to rush into any huge commitment until we know where we're heading."

"I agree. The marriage idea was dumb. I just wanted to hang on to you."

"Right, I understand. And if I went for the idea and actually started planning a wedding, you'd probably get scared and run off."

"No way."

She smiled and we kissed across the table as the waitress came hurrying over with glasses of water, her head turned toward another table. She nailed me on the chin with a glass, and half the water hit Kelly in the face. We did manage to avoid broken glass and blood, and laughed as the waitress apologized.

Kelly wanted to explore the running off theme further. "I don't know, Jackson. You have a motorcycle, a sailboat. You have the transportation to escape any number of ways."

"That's true, I guess. I just can't see taking off if you wanted to marry me. Nope."

We agreed to drop the marriage talk until she was at least finished with her undergraduate work. "And then we'll see. We'll see where we are."

"Fair enough. I wonder where I'll be in four years."

"Still debating what to do this fall?"

"Yeah. Some days I decide to definitely go to JC and play ball. Other days I feel pretty content on the boat and think the sailing life is for me. I'm sort of torn between my old path and my new one."

"That implies you want to make a career out of sailing somehow."

"Yeah, that's true. I haven't really thought it through completely, but after living aboard this summer, I can't ever imagine living very far from the sea. I love being on a boat, and at the very least I'll need to have the ocean in sight."

She was shaking her head in a nice way. "My Jackson, the sailor. You've really been bitten by the sea bug."

"I guess I have," I admitted with a smile. Our food arrived and I dug into my seafood chowder. It felt good, putting into words this feeling I'd had for weeks.

"Reminds me of the way you were so dedicated to basketball," she added, using her fork for emphasis. "I know you still love the game, and might play in college. But it's so competitive. Only a few hundred or so of all the top players make it to the NBA. With sailing, there are a million things you could do."

I nodded, looking out the window at the bay and Sandy Hook in the distance. Basketball and track had been pretty disappointing. Not the sports—I loved playing ball and soaring over the bar and all that stuff. No, I was disappointed that I didn't get a scholarship, have a better season, jump a little higher.

With sailing, it was different. It was hard to start from scratch after developing my basketball game for so many years. But Conrad noted that my balance, coordination, and general athleticism helped me on a boat. Likewise, the discipline I'd developed over the years—practicing moves until they became instinctive, reading books and applying the knowledge on the court—helped me pick up sailing much quicker than most novices.

I was also hungry to improve as a sailor, whereas I didn't feel I was going to get a whole lot better as a basketball player. I could compete with most college players I'd gone against in pickup games, but every now and then I'd encounter a really good player who humbled me. And of course I'd been playing for years against Thaddeus, who was downright embarrassing. For weeks I'd had a vague feeling I was approaching the end of the road as a basketball player, and it made practicing on my own challenging for the first time since…I could remember.

"Hello?" Kelly said. "You were far away."

"Distant basketball courts."

She put her hand on mine. "You don't have to make a decision right now. There's no reason you couldn't play basketball in college. It's just you were always so into the NBA…"

"Yeah, that was the dream. And it's not going to come true…Duh, right?"

She smiled but it was a little sad. "You're not the first guy with unrealistic aspirations as an athlete. There's a lot of that going around."

"True. Anyway, it's hard to give up my hoop dreams after all those years of practice, but I was just thinking that some of it translates pretty well to boats. One difference is that with sailing I don't have a dream of greatness and don't want to compete. Being part of the crew, taking orders from some blowhard, racing boats—none of that appeals to me at all."

"You didn't really seem to like the team aspects of basketball as much as playing on your own," she said.

"Pretty good observation. The difference is that I was always imagining other players around me when I was practicing basketball alone, whereas sailing by myself is fine just as it is. I don't imagine racing against other boats or having passengers aboard, although I'm cool with passengers. It's just that I'm content with the boat and the wonders of the ocean, and I can't imagine that ever disappointing me the way basketball did."

"Jackson, the sailor man."

"Could be." I looked at my watch. "We should get going."

"We should, but not back to my house. I had an argument with my dad—I don't think it'll shock you to know it was about you, Mr. O'Connell. Plus, I'm heading off on my own soon, and I'm feeling rebellious. Is there enough room on your boat for both of us tonight?"

"I'll have to check, Kels, but I think I can squeeze you in. I really do."

.   .   .

Before heading to the marina, we went to a club she'd heard about in Manasquan. She took a junior college class with a bouncer who could get us inside, she explained, and she didn't think they'd card us at the bar if we could get past the door.

She jokingly accused me of club-hopping while we were apart, knowing that I wasn't much for nightlife if it didn't involve her. "You were out tripping the light fantastic every night, weren't you?"

"Tripping over stands at the boatyard because I was thinking about you," I said as we walked through the warm evening. It was true, and it pleased her to hear it. She squeezed my hand and put her head on my shoulder.

Her bouncer friend had no neck and was built like a linebacker. He was obviously disappointed to see that Kelly had brought her boyfriend along. Still, she managed to charm him into letting us inside Club Caribbean. The place was packed, mostly with college students. We looked about the same age, and it helped that both of us were tall.

Kelly soon started moving to the beat of the loud music, and talked to me even though I couldn't hear her. The band wasn't going to make anyone forget Bon Jovi, though they weren't terrible.

Looking around, I noticed that Club Caribbean had a nautical theme. A smiling shark dangled from the ceiling, and huge mirrors on the walls were cut into the shape of marine life, including whales, sea lions, and various fish. The place was okay for people watching. We saw a few spiked mohawks, fearsome piercings, and meandering tattoos. The revolving light in the middle made everyone look like they were wanted by the FBI.

We danced to a few songs, then left. I decided to leave the motorcycle in the parking lot for the night. It looked to be fairly safe, and the storage shed was on the other side of the marina. We walked over to *Morning Sun* and I gave Kelly the two-second tour and dropped my helmet in the V-berth.

"Let's walk the beach," she suggested. We walked about a half-mile along the lighted boardwalk, then onto the sand

and to the edge of the dark ocean. We held hands and admired the soft roar of the surf and the nearly full moon.

"Maybe I'll get a tattoo tomorrow," she said, breaking the romantic mood. "That would freak my dad out."

"Good idea," I said. "How about a heart placed on your shoulder blade with the words, 'Jackson and Kelly forever.'"

"That's almost as much commitment as marriage, though it does have a certain ring," she laughed. "I'm surprised you haven't got a tattoo, now that you're a boat guy. You afraid of a little pain, big tough sailor man?"

"Nah, I thought about it, but I like the look of my bod too much," I admitted. "Maybe I'll get a little one someday, but nothing that covers up the ripped muscles."

"Vanity, thy name is Jackson," she said. "But I do like your ripped muscles. And now that you're tan, ooh-la-la, you look fantastic."

"So do you."

"Sure, but I don't look tan. I guess I'm fated to my natural alabaster complexion."

"Looks good to me," I said, stepping closer.

"Uh-oh, Jackson's moving in for the kill," she said, then she turned and ran, laughing. I chased after her and tackled her on the sand, and we kissed for a while.

Suddenly she jumped up and ran toward the waves. I followed her. She sat on an old log and began shedding her clothes.

"Geez, Kels," I said, looking around. I didn't see anyone but I was still sort of worried. "You sure you want to do that? There's people around."

"Oh, come on, Jackson, it's the beach. People wear bathing suits, which is no different than underwear, if you think about it. Let's go skinny dipping."

"You're in a wild mood."

"I am," she agreed. "I feel free!" With that she threw off the last of her clothes and ran into the ocean.

I looked around again. I took off my running shoes and shirt, checked the area one last time, and dropped my shorts. I was sure the lights of a dozen police cars were going to blaze to life any second, but what the hell.

I ran into the surf and dove under a wave, feeling a little better when I was beneath the water and no one could see what I had on—or rather, didn't have on. I swam over to Kelly. She laughed and put her arms around me and gave me a salty kiss, and I forgot about the cops.

Afterward, we dressed quickly and walked back to *Morning Sun*. We were both anxious to get out of our wet and sandy clothes. I gave Kelly a towel and some sweats, and she dried off and changed. She was still shivering, though, so I fired up the space heater and told her to get into the sleeping bag on the bunk.

Curled in the bag, her shivering began to subside. I crawled in and put my arms around her, and we warmed up together.

About three in the morning the wind started blowing pretty hard; the rocking motion woke me up, but I went right back to sleep. Soon after Kelly sat up quickly, which made the boat rock even more. Her eyes were wide and she was pale.

"I don't feel good," she said. "Can you stop the boat from rocking?"

"No," I laughed, "that's what boats do in the wind. Just relax."

She sat there for a moment, then yelled, "Bathroom!" I could tell she wasn't going to make it, so I looked around the cabin for a container. I grabbed the nearest useful object—my motorcycle helmet.

She took it in her hands, bent forward, and hurled. The contents of her stomach filled the helmet most of the way; another couple of inches and it would have leaked over the rim. I rubbed her back and gave her some water, then went up top and dumped the puke out of the helmet. Her breathing was irregular and deep, and she had a couple of false alarms. She insisted on walking up to the women's room at the marina while I went to the men's room and cleaned out the evil-smelling helmet.

The wind died down and Kelly bravely decided to give the boat another try. I gave her a glass of water and she took deep breaths. She was still shaky, so I tried to help by massaging her shoulders and back. After a while she said she felt better and crawled back into the sleeping bag.

She was half-asleep when she turned to me and smiled. "Jackson, you gave me your helmet to puke in," she whispered contentedly. "Now that's true love."

THIRTEEN

*"To me, the sea is like a person—like a child
that I've known a long time. It sounds crazy,
I know, but when I swim in the sea I talk to
it. I never feel alone when I'm out there."*

—Gertrude Ederle,
first woman to swim the English Channel

Kelly had a summer job as a go-fer at a law firm, so we both had to be up early on Monday. We only had a few hours sleep and knew we were going to be dragging. I drove her back home to Highland as the sun was rising. The cold motorcycle ride—along with caffeinated beverages—helped to revive us.

I was being especially careful because Kelly refused to wear the motorcycle helmet, even after I cleaned it again. She checked herself once in my rearview mirror when we were stopped at a red light. "Who is that appallingly pale ghost on the back of your bike?" she asked. "What a homely witch."

"She looks great to me," I said on cue. She sighed and rested her head on my back. I saw her long brown hair streaming wildly behind us when I looked in the mirror a few times, and I noticed some early commuters staring at us. I don't know if we looked crazy or pretty cool.

When we reached her house, I offered to come in and help explain, but she kissed me and told me to get going, that she could handle her father without my assistance. "I still feel bad about the way he barked at you graduation night," she said. "He just doesn't understand that I'm responsible for myself—or irresponsible, as the case may be. I seem to end up with my head in the toilet on all our big dates."

We both laughed. "But Kels," I corrected, "the bathroom on a boat is called the head."

She rolled her big brown eyes. "Don't get nautical on me, Jackson," she said. "My parents are going to assume I'm a tramp because I spent the night with you, and you think I'm going to mention that I had my head in the head? They'd think naughty, not nautical."

We laughed and kissed again. As I drove off I thought I saw a curtain move in her parents' upstairs bedroom, and felt momentarily guilty that I was leaving Kelly to take the heat by herself. She was right, though. She could handle her old man just fine, and I'd already taken enough crap from him.

Fortunately, I had an easy morning at the marina. Conrad arranged for the Travelift to put three boats I'd finished in the water, and bring two others out. The Travelift looked like a huge praying mantis on wheels, and the operator did most of the work. All I had to do was help him with the straps and lines and take the boats to their slips when they were in the water.

Even so, Conrad noticed that I was dragging. "Looks like you tied one on last night," he said. "Either that or someone beat the hell outta ya."

"No, I only had a couple of beers," I explained. "It was a late date, and I had to get home early."

"So someone did beat the hell outta ya," he winked. "Why don't you take a nap after lunch? Come back around three. I don't want you starting on these boats when you can't see straight and you're reminiscing about your gal."

I thanked him and walked slowly back to *Morning Sun*, thinking that Conrad could be a great boss…some days. It helped that he knew I worked hard and was trustworthy. He mentioned that I'd already lasted longer than any employee he'd ever had.

I ate some bread, cheese, and fruit and washed it down with water. It was a little hot, so I took off my shirt. Reclining on my bunk, hands laced behind my head, I enjoyed the breeze from my small fan and grew drowsy from my full stomach. I hadn't played ball in a couple of days, and for the first time I didn't feel guilty about it. My usual pattern was to miss a day, then practice hard after work the next day, get motivated to take my game to the next level and all that. I'd go hard a few days, then skip another day or two.

Was it so bad to be interested in something besides basketball? Kelly was always encouraging me to expand my horizons. That sounded fine, but it was sure humbling. I had some serious skills on the court, was a top player almost everywhere I went. And on a boat I was a rookie just learning the game.

On the upside, the dedication that made me a good basketball player was translating fairly well to sailing. Plus, I didn't feel so bad about starting from scratch when I looked at a gorgeous boat bobbing in the marina, or when I sailed out to the ocean. It was just a new game, and I was improving. Maybe you can learn anything if you stick with it and don't let the Putdown Predators change your course.

I dozed for a few minutes, until the sound of loud laughter half woke me. For a moment I thought I might be dreaming, but I woke completely when I heard the laughter coming closer.

I stood, pulled back the hatch, and looked around. A young businessman was striding purposefully up the dock. He had thinning blond hair, a thick neck, and was on the chunky side. His suit was basic business—gray pinstripe, with a crisp white shirt and a light blue tie. One moment he'd look serious, and the next he'd let loose a crazy laugh, sort of funny bordering on scary. Clearly he was at the end of his rope, and a few moments later he was at the end of the dock.

He stripped off his jacket and flung it behind him. The

jacket looked expensive to me, although with my limited wardrobe, I'm no expert. Anyway, by sheer luck the jacket landed on top of a piling rather than in the water. Not that an oily piling was much better, but maybe it wasn't ruined.

Next he pulled off his tie and flung it into the air. No luck this time, it went right in the water. He ripped off his shirt, kicked off his shoes—plop, plop—let loose a final laugh, walked to the end of a finger pier, and dove into the water.

I scrambled up the steps, jumped off *Morning Sun,* and ran down the dock. I could seen him swimming strongly, and was a little relieved but still concerned. He didn't look like he was in shape. Sure enough, I saw his strokes become labored. My run had taken me near the end of the dock, and I had a decision to make: I could watch him and hope for the best; I could go out on the same finger pier and swim after him. Or I could save time and dive over the motorboat at the end of the dock.

Other than playing in a few pickup games in the evening after work, I hadn't attempted anything truly athletic since my failed attempt to clear six-foot-nine in the state high jump championships. That failure made up my mind, and I increased my speed, deciding to go for it.

I took a little hop at the end of the pier, sort of a rolling jump stop to control my momentum and convert my speed into height. By the time I noticed the couple lounging in the cockpit of the motorboat, I was already committed. I sprang into the air above the boat. The woman screamed as I eclipsed the sun and her boyfriend looked up in time to see my downward arc. I think it looked riskier than it was. I knew I could clear a standard open motorboat with ease.

I knifed into the water a good six feet beyond the boat and swam underwater for as long as my breath held. When I surfaced I looked back at the motorboat. The couple was standing and looking at me, the woman with her mouth open, and I waved, half-expecting them to respond with curses and threats. Instead the guy pointed at me and yelled, "That was tight, dude! You scared the crap out of me, but that was tight!"

I was almost parallel to the struggling businessman. He was about twenty yards away. I swam toward him as fast as possible. He was trying to tread water, but doing more splashing than stroking, and I saw fatigue and panic in his eyes.

Finally I reached him. I didn't want to take a chance on him pulling me under, so I came up behind him, put my left arm diagonally over his chest, and my left hip under his lower back. He struggled for a second, and I told him to relax. I side-stroked toward the remains of a pier twenty yards away, much closer than the marina docks. I figured we could rest there and then swim back when he regained his strength.

What was left of the pier angled sharply into the water from a pair of crooked pilings. He groped the rotting wooden boards, breathing hard. I went around to the other side and rested myself. He was a load to haul along and didn't have enough energy to even kick.

When his breathing was almost back to normal, he gave an abbreviated version of his crazy laugh and said, "Good day for a swim, huh?"

"Are you okay?"

"I am now. Never been better."

"Well, it looked like you were drowning," I said. "And it looked like you wanted to."

"No, no, I wasn't trying to kill myself," he protested. "Not really. I guess I wouldn't have minded at first, but not once I started swimming. Mostly I just wanted to jump in the ocean. I've been thinking about it for days."

He wanted to jump in the ocean. I thought about punching him in the snot locker. He saw the look on my face and read my violent thoughts.

"Sorry to put you out," he said quickly. "I mean, I suppose I was borderline suicidal. This was a cry for help, in a sense. But I'm okay now…I'll tell you, though, I would have committed suicide if I stayed at my job another day. It was killing me, killing me!"

"What did you do?" I asked, feeling more curious than angry.

"I sell insurance for The Good Life," he said. "Sold insurance—past tense."

"Why didn't you just quit and go home?"

"That's a long story," he said, letting his legs drift out behind him with the current. He was starting to enjoy his day at the beach. "Basically, I've been unhappy for a long time and felt compelled to do something dramatic. I lost it with a customer yesterday. Told her she was crazy to buy insurance from us. And this morning I shoved my boss into the coffee machine. He fired me, but I was going to quit anyway at that point. I'll never take crap from him or anyone else again."

"What are you going to do now?"

The wild laugh again. Some splashing.

"I don't have any idea! I got a big bonus check last week, so I have enough to live on for a while. That bonus was what made me look around at my life. After a sale you're supposed to feel good, like you accomplished something, but I just felt empty. Sure, I made a few bucks, but you know, when I was a kid, I didn't see myself living for a lousy insurance bonus. I stayed up all that night, just thinking. And I concluded that I was going to change my life."

"I guess you did."

"Yeah, but it took me a week to work up to it, and I had to make a big scene to go through with it…Part of me was pretty scared, part of me was depressed, and part of me was hopeful, you know? What's your name, anyway?"

"Jackson."

"I'm Frank," he said, and we shook hands across the wrecked pier. "Thanks for coming after me. I mean, I would have been okay, I just needed to catch my breath. But I appreciate your concern."

"Why didn't you go down to the beach?" I asked.

"That would have been easier—and cleaner." I was thinking about Kelly's vomit, motor oil, and other gross stuff that goes into the water around a marina.

"I used to share a boat on this dock with a friend," he said. "I still have a key. I don't know, it was sort of for old-time's sake." He'd been through enough, so I didn't argue with him. I felt good about what I'd done—the way he was struggling, he would have been trying to catch his breath underwater in another minute.

"Boy, is my wife going to be pissed," he continued. "I can't talk to her about heavy subjects, she just gets angry, but I have no choice now. 'Honey, I've had an early mid-life crisis.'" He laughed and threw his head back in the water. "She's going to lose it! She was the main reason I was so afraid to make a change…She'll probably leave me, but so be it. I can't go back to my old life. Or The Good Life. Hah!"

First Kelly, now this guy. Everyone was a comedian today.

When he was done laughing, I asked him if he was strong enough to swim back to the marina dock. He said sure. I told him to take it slow, I'd be right behind him if he had any trouble. He started off strong and was headed in the right direction. I was mildly surprised. I half-expected him to give a mad cry and try to swim to England or somewhere.

He had to stop three times to rest, during which he held onto my shoulders while I treaded water. When he reached the dock, he couldn't pull himself up—I tried to push him but had no leverage, so I hopped out and dragged him onto the concrete like a big fish. The water had thoroughly soaked through his business pants and they clung to his legs. He was so tired he just flopped over on his back and panted.

For the first time I noticed the lunch crowd staring at us from outside the marina gate and through the windows of the restaurants. The couple from the motorboat was standing in the middle of a group and pointing at me. Great. Just beautiful.

Sure enough, a cop showed up a few minutes later. "Time to get going, Frank," I said. He managed to sit up. "You got a car here?"

"Yeah, thanks for reminding me." He patted his pants and was relieved to find his keys were still in his pocket. He turned his attention back to me. "You live down here, Jackson?"

"Yup, I'm on that sailboat over there."

"That's the life. I envy you."

"It's growing on me. I wasn't so sure at first—it was kind of weird after always living in a house—but now I can't imagine ever living anyplace but aboard a boat. I can imagine living on a bigger one."

"Maybe I'll sell my house and buy a sailboat."

I wasn't sure I should be encouraging him. His wife might name me as a factor in the divorce…But what the hell. He was as brave as he was crazy. "There are worse ways to live," I shrugged.

"Tell me about it. Listen, never change, Jackson. Appreciate what you've got here. I can see you're very young, but you're also as free as anyone I've ever known. Don't surrender that lightly, buddy."

A marina security guard let the cop in the gate and he strolled down to us. He glowered and towered. "What's going on here?" he asked at last.

"Just taking a dip," Frank replied.

"Yeah, in a thousand dollar suit," the cop snorted. Then he looked at me. "And I hear you're Superman. 'It's a bird! It's a plane! It's the kid living on a sailboat!'"

I couldn't help but laugh. I said, "I knew I could jump over the boat, officer. I didn't mean to scare them."

"Yeah, well, they were as much thrilled as scared, but it sounded like a risky stunt. How did you know you'd clear the boat? Or that there wasn't a dingy on the far side? You could have hurt them, not to mention yourself."

"Don't mean to brag, sir, but I finished second in the state high school high jump championships, cleared six-nine, and there was no way I was going to hurt myself."

The cop whistled and nodded. He was a big guy, moved like a cat, and was obviously an ex-jock of some sort. It felt good to impress him, even if I did exaggerate my high jump record slightly. He inclined his head down the dock. I followed him until we were out of earshot. Frank wasn't going anywhere fast.

"The couple in the boat and a few other witnesses said you pulled him out. That true?"

"Yeah," I nodded. "He was starting to struggle so I went after him."

"Good going," he said, patting my shoulder. "That's your good deed for the day. Now I have to figure out what to do with him. Is he suicidal?"

"He was, sort of. I think he's okay now."

The cop nodded. "So you're Superman," he said, and then turned and looked at Frank. "And I guess that makes him the Little friggin' Mermaid." We both laughed. I turned to go to my boat while he walked back over to Frank.

Frank wasn't in a quiet mood, and I could hear him telling the cop his sad story. It sounded like the cop was counseling him, telling him some organizations he might want to contact. He probably couldn't arrest Frank if he wanted to. There aren't any laws against laughing madly, swimming badly, and ruining a nice suit.

I dried off and returned to my bunk. I was a little wired and couldn't go right to sleep, so I thought about Frank the former businessman. Only a couple of years ago I thought adults had all the answers. My parents proved me wrong, and people like Frank confirmed that fact. No one had all the answers, not even close. Although Gerry might have rounded up one or two.

I thought about Frank telling me I'm lucky. I'd been feeling sorry for myself because my big basketball dream was turning small, at best. But other than that, everything was pretty good in my life, even great in some ways. Maybe I was lucky.

FOURTEEN

*"Home is the sailor, home from the sea, and
the hunter home from the hill."*

—Robert Louis Stevenson

In mid-July I graduated from the *Sunfish* to *Morning Sun*. Conrad took me out the first two times. He grunted his approval at the improvements I'd made to the interior and the overall cleanliness. I'd read enough to know that while the sailing principles were the same for any size boat, the larger ones were far more complex.

"A lot can go wrong out there," Conrad said, inclining his head toward the Atlantic. "So you want a backup for every system. Lose your rudder, pull out the spare. Lose your mast, know how to rig the boom into a simple sail. Keep extra sails, extra fuel, extra lines. A life raft and emergency supplies if you plan to venture out beyond swimming distance. And learn everything there is to know about your motor."

Innocently, I asked if all of the larger sailboats used engines. That sent Conrad into a rage. "Some of those damn purists won't use a motor, they'll tell you that's not sailing," he railed. "But they'll sure as hell beg for a tow when the wind dies. I don't know how many tows I've given over the years to purists. Too many, that's for sure."

The first time we took out *Morning Sun* was a fine day, and I was able to get a feel for how she handled. The second time the wind was blowing nearly twenty knots, kicking up whitecaps, and jangling halyards against masts; the marina sounded like a bad calypso band. While I loosened the lines, Conrad yelled over the racket, "Now we'll do some sailing!"

I'd noticed that he was a different man on the water. Obviously, his long gray hair and beard seemed appropriate for a sailor, whereas he looked out of place in a business setting. It's true that he was just as bossy at times, but his tone was different on the boat, more directive and less abusive. I mean, half the time when I asked a question in his shop or the yard, he'd cuss me, answer gruffly, and look annoyed at my stupidity. He never did that when we were sailing. No, he'd listen patiently and answer calmly, making sure I understood. When he wasn't instructing me, he kept quiet and looked around at the sea. He seemed content, even happy at times. On shore, he tended to intimidate people right out of his life, not to mention his shop.

Once I was aboard he let me take the helm. He checked over the boat, took a quick look under the hatch to make sure everything was secured down below, then made himself comfortable with a couple of deck cushions.

When I was a quarter mile beyond the breakwater, he had me head into the wind, cut the engine, and raise the mainsail. He took over the wheel, and turned to port as soon as I raised the sail. *Morning Sun* immediately heeled over; I was thrown off balance—I knew he did it intentionally—and had to hold on to the mast with one hand. I managed to tie off the halyard with my other hand.

"Well done!" Conrad complimented. "Maybe we'll make a sailor out of you yet!"

Back in the cockpit, he had me take the wheel again. "Bring her about," he said, and I changed our direction to the northeast, released the starboard sheet, hauled in the port sheet to bring the jib around to that side, then adjusted the boom vang so the mainsail was at a better angle to the wind. He ordered a dozen more tacks, and I had to repeat the same procedure; my speed improved significantly by the end, although he didn't mention it.

Next he flung one of the floating cushions off the starboard side. "Oops, someone fell overboard. Go get 'em," he said. I did a figure eight maneuver, which I'd read about and practiced mentally, then used a boat-hook to scoop up the cushion by the straps.

"Jibe works well on a rescue, too," he noted. "Faster, but a little more dangerous, especially in high winds. If you have a crew, make sure someone acts as a spotter for the person in the water." We practiced a few more times.

Finally he had me go forward on the bow and change the jib, the front sail. My haphazard sailing wardrobe—sneakers, black polyester workout pants, sweatshirt, cheap blue raincoat—was a little wet from wave spray at that point. When I moved forward, the rising and dipping motion of the bow was much more noticeable, and so was the spray, which soon had me soaked. At one point I turned my dripping face and saw Conrad, warm and dry in his yellow heavy weather suit. He smiled and winked, clearly pleased at my discomfort. It was like riding a bucking horse through a car wash.

We were flying with the large jib; the wind curved it until it looked like half a balloon was driving the boat. The medium one put us in better control. The small one—the storm jib—wasn't necessary, but Conrad had me raise it anyway for practice.

"If you're going to be sailing a boat this size alone, you'll want to get self-steering," he said when I returned to the cockpit. "You obviously don't want the boat turning out of control while you're forward working the sails. Good to arrange it so all your lines run back to the cockpit, too, save you from going forward."

"Right," I nodded, able to see his reasoning.

"This boat, twenty-four feet or so, is really about as big as you want to sail single-handed," he added. "Thirty feet at the outside. Some experienced sailors will go as large as thirty-five, thirty-six feet, but experienced or not, that's almost too much boat for one man."

"Or woman," I added, thinking of Kelly. Conrad threw me a funny look. I'd read about some very good women sailors, though, and I knew Kelly Armstead could do whatever she set her mind to. She might take up sailing large boats just to piss him off.

We headed back in after three hours. I was tired—sailing was more of a workout than I'd ever imagined. I could tell Conrad was tired, too, although he was mostly sitting around giving orders. The wind let up a bit by the time we reached the river leading to the marina. Conrad had been silent for a while, but when the sails were down and we were motoring slowly up the river, he gave me one last lesson.

"A sailboat," he said, "is a kite on top, a fish on bottom, and a sailor in between. Keep the kite under control, the fish in the water, and the sailor prepared."

. . .

I continued practicing by myself aboard *Morning Sun*, taking her out at least four times a week, honing my sailing and navigation skills. Every time out I added some small but helpful knowledge such as using bungee cords to keep the sails orderly on deck, or cutting the engine well before

I reached my slip. And I soon felt confident enough to invite passengers aboard.

The first two were my sister Shannon and her friend, Lisa Snelling. I still talked to Shannon on the phone every other week or so, and Kelly and I took her to lunch in Red Bank a few weeks earlier. She was interested in my sailing adventures and made me promise to take her out.

The first Sunday in August was the day. They called before they left in the morning and I waited for them in the shade of a tree next to the marina parking lot. Finally I saw them pull into the lot, Mom at the wheel of a new-looking car. Shannon and her friend were smiling, towels around their shoulders, obviously excited about a day at the shore. Mom looked like she was trying to smile but having trouble.

"How's it going?" I asked. I hugged Shannon and Mom—she was a little more receptive than she'd been at Granny's funeral—and shook hands when I was introduced to Lisa. She and Shannon made quite a pair; both were very pretty, though different types: Shannon had dark hair and eyes and the same pale complexion as Kelly, while Lisa was strawberry blond with lightly freckled skin. Still, they were about the same size, wore their hair in the same carefree bob, flashed perfect smiles, and shared a rowdy enthusiasm. If you didn't know better, you might take them for sisters.

"Jackson, why don't you let the girls go down and look at the boats, then come back and talk to me," Mom said. Something in her tone told me she was upset.

"Sure," I shrugged, and led the girls over to the marina gate. They each wore pastel one-piece bathing suits and lugged backpacks full of girl stuff. I opened the gate, pointed out *Morning Sun*, and told them to feel free to walk around the docks and explore, I'd be along in a few minutes.

Back at the car, Mom lit a cigarette. Always a sign that she was worried. "Nice car," I said, patting the hood. "New?"

"Yes, I've sold some houses and we're doing wonderfully...considering," she said. "Look, I got a call from your father." She said "father" like it was a curse. "He's trying to act like nothing happened because he's sober for a change."

Nodding, I said, "I think he's trying to start fresh." I knew where she was coming from, though. When he called me "son" it rubbed me the wrong way during our last conversation, and he probably made a similarly casual, all-in-the-family reference that torqued off Mom.

"Well, he can start fresh all he wants, but I don't need to hear him talking in that tone he uses now, like he's been away on a business trip," she said, flicking an ash out the window. I had to move my sandaled foot out of the way. "It just made me so angry. Then he had the nerve to want to talk with Shannon. After what he put her through."

"Yeah, he's trying too hard to get back in our lives," I nodded. "Did you let him talk to her?"

She looked up at me, and even though she was wearing dark sunglasses, I knew she was giving me the evil eye. "Now why would I do that? What kind of mother would I be to let that...that...phony bastard hurt my daughter again?"

"He doesn't want to hurt her," I said softly, and she blew a plume of smoke at me and shook her head.

"You always take his side; I don't know why I try to talk to you about this."

That got me a little mad. Just because I hadn't gone along with her and her lawyer when they tried to nail him to the cross during the divorce, she thought of me as a traitor. "I'm not taking his side," I replied, "I just don't think he's a monster. Why shouldn't Shannon talk to him? What's the big deal? She's old enough to handle it."

She gave me a look of disgust and rolled up her window. Then she rolled it down. "I'll be back for the girls at eight," she said. "You be careful with them on that boat, and have them out here ready to go."

"Sure, see ya, Mom," I said. She ignored me and rolled up the window as she backed away.

Walking back to the marina, I took some deep breaths. I hated thinking about my parents' problems. The problem now was that Mom wasn't the forgiving sort. She wanted to forget she'd ever known Dad, and he was trying to make peace. Maybe he was a little clumsy about it, but he was trying.

I decided that it was too nice a day to think about them. Walking down the ramp to the floating dock, I saw Shannon and Lisa talking to an acquaintance of mine named Ben Fredrickson. He lived a few boats over aboard *Dancin' Bare*. He was kind of old, in his late forties, but he liked younger women, and it was obvious he was flirting with my sister and her friend.

"Hey Ben," I nodded. "Telling some lies to the ladies?"

"Listen to you," he laughed. Turning back to Shannon and Lisa, he jerked a thumb at me and said, "Sailing a couple of months and he feels free to criticize an old salt like me." I could tell he immediately regretted using the word "old," which he was trying to de-emphasize. "You girls gonna trust Jackson out there on the big bad ocean?" he added hurriedly. "Why don't you come along with me? I'll keep the water outta your lungs."

They laughed, slightly uncomfortable, and moved closer to me as they declined the invitation. He smiled and waved and went back to his boat. We walked around to the docks where they kept the larger sailboats. I just liked to look at them; something about the sleek lines, the high masts, and the bright reflections in the water appealed to me. Shannon and Lisa asked me a few questions, and I told them about the marina and sailing and the characters like Ben.

I'd met a few other live-aboards, although most of them were very private and kept to themselves. I mentioned them as we walked back and passed their boats. Chris was a retired naval officer who lived on *Dream Catcher* and liked to fish. Dreena had sailed across the Atlantic on the *Salty Lady* and was planning to check out the Caribbean this winter. And Ray was a guy about Conrad's age who lived aboard *Idle Ours*. He told me he took up sailing last summer, after his wife left him.

"I've never seen Ray take his boat out," I said quietly, knowing how sound travels across the water. "To be honest, I don't think he sails at all. I think he just likes living on a boat."

"This is so awesome," Lisa giggled. "I gotta get my parents to buy a sailboat."

Back on *Morning Sun*, I gave them the quick tour. I stowed their packs, handed them life jackets, and went over the basics. I thought about taking them out on the *Sunfish*, but decided it was too small for three. Besides, the day was calm and clear, so I wasn't concerned.

They lathered on the suntan oil as I motored out past the breakwater. I raised the sails, and the light breeze pushed us along slowly. I let Shannon take the tiller, and it was obvious she loved the experience. "I'm going to visit you more often," she said with a hearty laugh. "You have to teach me to sail!"

"Promise to take me with you," Lisa said. "If it's okay with your brother." She smiled across at me. "Is it all right if I come back, Jackson?"

"Sure, anytime," I said. "But I'm still learning myself. I don't know if I'm qualified to teach anyone yet."

"Oh, you could teach me," she said. Shannon gave her friend a surprised look. I was positive she liked me at that point, and it was flattering because she was so pretty...pretty young, too. Not even a sophomore yet.

We headed south along Point Pleasant Beach. Sunbathers were out early, and Lisa and Shannon discussed their afternoon plans on the beach. I had Lisa take the tiller for a while. She enjoyed steering as well, but I could tell the boat was moving too slowly for their taste. So I took the helm, brought her around, and headed back toward the marina.

The wind picked up on our return, and *Morning Sun* began to heel slightly. Shannon was at the tiller again. I was on the starboard side, sitting opposite Lisa, who became wide-eyed as the port side of the boat began dipping toward the water. We needed to balance the boat, so I reached my hand out to her.

"Come over here," I said. Lisa took my hand, ducked under the mast, and plopped down next to me—with her left leg touching my right. She pressed up against me and acted scared, even though we were sailing along just fine. I looked over at Shannon, handling the boat like a pro, and she smiled and rolled her eyes.

Once back at my slip, I gave them their packs and suggested lunch at a burger place on Manasquan Beach. The girls were hungry and quickly agreed. We walked over and talked about what they'd been doing over the summer and the dreaded return to school in less than a month. My own plans were unclear, so I tried to keep the conversation focused on them.

We sat under an umbrella and turned our chairs to face the ocean; Lisa sat between Shannon and I. The breeze kept it from being too hot. After we ordered, Lisa excused herself to use the bathroom.

"She likes you," Shannon said when her friend was out of earshot.

"Yeah, I got that," I said with a shrug.

"How're you and Kelly doing?"

"Fair, I guess. We're great some days, and other days she talks about us in the past tense. She wants to do the 'friends' thing when she goes to Princeton."

"The kiss of death."

"Yeah. Plus, her father is pushing her to break up with me. She acts like she's a rebel and could care less what he thinks, but I can tell he has a lot of influence over her."

"So you should hook up with Lisa." She smiled up at me as she sipped her Coke.

"Nah," I said, although I must admit I was excited by the prospect. "She's your age. Too young for me."

"Women mature faster, so she's just about right," Shannon smirked. "She's nice and really smart. I'll bet you'd get along great."

"Maybe," I said. "How about you, Miss Fixer-upper? You seeing anyone?"

"Yeah, sort of. He's named Brian. He's a cute football player, but not too smart."

"Smart's your thing?"

"Beats stupid."

"True."

"So what did you and Mom talk about?" she asked.

"The Great Satan," I said.

She nodded and looked at the ocean. "She was really mad when he called."

"Did you know he wanted to talk to you?"

"Yeah, I could tell by Mom's reaction," she shrugged. "I'll talk to him sometime, I guess. Not that we'd have much to talk about. School. Work. Why he was an alcoholic idiot."

"Come on, Shannon, he's been sober for over a year," I said. "What happened to forgive and forget?"

"Guess I'm not as forgiving as you."

"Or Mom has you brainwashed."

"She tries, but I can think for myself, thanks."

"Sorry."

She sighed. "I'll probably get around to forgiving him," she said. "I know he's sorry and he's working at staying sober and being a dad. Guess it's not too late."

"I'm going to see him when he comes out East later this month," I said. "I know Mom doesn't want to see him— and doesn't want you to see him. But think it over and call me. You could figure a way to come out here when he visits, if you want."

"Okay," she shrugged. Lisa returned and of course we changed the subject. After lunch we did the boardwalk, played some games in the arcades. They sunbathed while I hit baseballs at the batting cage, then we all went swimming. The tide was coming in and the waves were perfect for bodysurfing. I had a few long rides.

We went back to the boat when the sun started its dive. For some reason, they found it very funny when I called and ordered a pizza. "Pizza delivery to your boat," Shannon laughed while shaking her head. "You've got it made here, bro."

"Well, they don't deliver right to the boat, I have to go up to the gate and get it," I said. "What's the big deal? They'll deliver a pizza just about anywhere."

We ate and watched the setting sun turn the water a deeper blue with flecks of orange. We listened to the gulls and the slap of small waves against the boats. The silence was nice and comfortable. After a while Lisa snugged her hand into mine, and Shannon pretended not to notice.

At ten to eight, Shannon said she should go up to the parking lot and look for Mom. Lisa told her she'd be along in a minute, and my sister gave her a knowing smile before hugging me goodbye.

Lisa went below to get her pack. I helped her step off the boat and onto the finger pier. She put her hands on my shoulders, and kept them there after she was safely on the pier. "I had a great day, Jackson. Thanks for everything."

"You're welcome," I said, looking into her eyes. I tried to think of something witty to say, but could only add, "It was nice to meet you."

"I'd like to see you again," she said. "Get my number from Shannon."

"Okay," I said, looking at her pretty face. She tilted her head slightly and leaned toward me, and of course I kissed her. I don't see how any guy could have resisted, and I know this guy couldn't.

FIFTEEN

*"With all of our running and
all of our cunning,
If we couldn't laugh
we would all go insane."*

—Jimmy Buffett

I called Lisa a few days later and asked her to a movie on Saturday. She said she'd love to go and we had a nice talk. Shannon was right, she was smart and mature. It was a little hard for me to think of a mere sophomore-to-be in those terms, especially after going out with Kelly for the last six months. Although Kelly was only eighteen, she sometimes acted closer to thirty.

Naturally I didn't mention to Lisa that she was Plan B, that'd I'd called Kelly first but she was leaving on a family vacation to Maine on Friday and would be gone the following week. Kelly asked me if I'd help her move to her dorm at Princeton when she got back, and I told her sure, no problem.

I felt a little slimy for not mentioning Lisa to Kelly, or Kelly to Lisa. Of course, Lisa might have known about my sort-of girlfriend from Shannon, and Kelly might not have cared if I saw someone else because she was leaving me behind anyway. Prior to this year I'd never had to worry about one girlfriend, much less two, and I was beginning to realize how complicated it could get.

The date went okay. Lisa's parents were nice, although a little apprehensive about the motorcycle, even though I now had a second helmet. Lisa pestered them until they relented. I promised to be careful. We were going to a mall less than a mile away through neighborhood streets, so they seemed somewhat reassured.

After the movie, we went for some dessert. Every now and then I'd think of Kelly and have a stab of guilt, but mostly I enjoyed getting to know Lisa. I wanted to get her back to *Morning Sun* and rock the boat a bit, but her parents told me to have her home by eleven, so there was no way.

Danny, Angelo, and Thaddeus came out for a sail the next day. We'd been talking about it all summer, and with Danny and Thaddeus leaving for college and Angelo getting busy with work and marriage, this was the last opportunity.

None of them had ever been sailing, though Angelo had done a lot of waterskiing with Debbie's family. Striding across the parking lot, wearing their usual shorts and sneakers and muscle shirts, they looked like they were heading off to play some pick-up basketball. Danny was carrying a picnic basket.

"'Ship ahoy' and 'thar she blows' and all that stuff," he said in greeting.

"Hey guys, glad you could make it." I led them to *Morning Sun* and showed them around.

"So this is where you've been hiding all summer," Thaddeus nodded, looking over my new home. "Pretty tight, Jax, but not a lot of space to spread out, you know? I think a guy my size might get stuck in that bathroom."

"It's called a head," I noted. "Guess it is a little small, but I'm used to it now. I never really knew how little space I needed until I started living on a boat."

"Beats living out of the brown beast," Danny said. "Where do you keep the basketball hoop?"

"How's married life?" I asked Angelo to change the subject.

"Great, except my father-in-law bosses me around at work," he said. "Other than that, we're just getting things for our apartment and enjoying married life…I told these guys, so I'll let you in on the news, too, Jackson. Debbie's expecting a baby."

"Hey, congratulations!" I said, shaking hands and acting surprised, and thinking Kelly really was smart.

"Yeah, he's reading *What to Expect When You're Expecting*, crap like that," Thaddeus said.

"It's not crap, Fly," Angelo said. "What would you know about having a kid?"

"I know he'd have a cool name like me, and probably some game."

"Thaddeus is going off to college, and here he is promoting illiteracy," Danny said.

"Thank Debbie and Rachel for making lunch," I said, nodding at the picnic basket.

"How do you know we didn't make it?"

"Educated guess."

While we were talking, I felt the wind pick up, and smiled. Just motoring around wouldn't be much fun. Thaddeus, meanwhile, grabbed the picnic basket from Danny and began poking around inside. "Let Uncle Thaddeus check out the goodies," he said. "What did the ladies pack for us? Hmmm. We have fried chicken, always nice. Pasta salad, fruit salad. And what is this? Brownies! This will work for me, what are you guys gonna eat?"

Most people would have thought he was kidding, but we'd seen Thaddeus eat. He wasn't a sloppy or fast eater, just consistent. He'd keep putting it away and looking around for more. All the basketball kept him slim. All summer he'd been traveling around to various camps to play and teach the game. Danny said his game was back to where it had been pre-meltdown.

"Wait for lunch, Fly," Angelo said, sounding like a father already. Danny smiled at me while they tussled some more. No one was going to say anything, but we all realized this might be the last time we saw each other together for a long time. Our basketball games at The High Court were all over, and we were going our separate ways.

I secured the lunch and drinks down below and went over the basics of sailing and safety. "We have three big guys aboard," I began.

"And one little Italian runt, is that what you're saying?" Angelo interrupted. Feigning tears, he added, "You know, small people have feelings, too."

"Just making the point that balancing the boat is important," I said. Danny and Thaddeus were laughing with Angelo and none of them were really listening. I went over the rest of the stuff as quickly as I could and they nodded along halfheartedly, wanting to get going. I was a little annoyed that they weren't paying as close attention as they should have been, but I let it pass. They didn't have the respect for the sea that I'd developed, and it wasn't something you could hand another person, like a set of car keys.

"We'll go out for an hour or so," I continued, "then come back, have lunch, head to the beach, whatever."

"Yes, Captain," Thaddeus said sarcastically. "I like the plan, especially the lunch part."

I motored us out of the marina and up the river. We passed a few boats and got a few stares. Thaddeus announced loudly, "Yes, I'm a black man and, yes, I'm a sailor! Haven't you people ever seen an African-American on a boat before?"

"Nah," said Danny, "it's not a race thing, it's our clothes. We don't look—what's the word?—nautical enough."

Angelo laughed as he noted the contrast between their casual muscle shirts and the crisp whites other sailors wore. "Without a doubt, we're the ghetto sailboat," he said.

Once past the breakwater, I cut the engine and had Danny and Thaddeus go forward and raise the sails. I'd noticed Angelo taking some deep breaths once we got into the ocean, looking a little scared, and I wanted to keep him safe in the cockpit.

While Angelo's newfound fear kept him in line, Thaddeus and Danny were screwing around as much as possible. It made me a little uncomfortable. I didn't say anything because they're my friends and I didn't want to spoil the day. Once the sails were up, I gave Thaddeus the helm to keep him occupied. I told him to head for a point on the horizon to the northeast.

Danny was bored after a few minutes. "Doesn't this tub go any faster?" he asked.

"If there's more wind."

"You should have gotten a speedboat so we could water-ski, have some fun."

"I'll keep your recreational preferences in mind next time I buy a boat."

He shrugged and walked over to Thaddeus. "Okay, my turn to steer, big fella," he said. "Let me have the tiller thing."

"No way," Thaddeus said. "I just got started. Besides, I feel like a pirate. 'Arg, me mates, let's find some gold!'" They continued to joke and argue with each other, and pretty much ignored me when I told them to cut it out. I'd never been the leader of any group, and especially not this one. Though I hate to admit it, I was basically the designated follower when I wasn't going my own way.

Soon they began jostling for the tiller for real, like they were going after a rebound. I tried to keep my tone casual as I told them again to stop. Angelo backed me up, but they ignored us. The wind had picked up, and our course was erratic as a result of the screwing around.

The wind also had *Morning Sun* heeling to starboard. This forced Thaddeus to bend his left leg while keeping his right straight for balance. Without thinking, Danny, still screwing around despite my reprimands, hip-checked Thaddeus in the right leg. Starting to fall, Fly pulled hard on the tiller to keep himself upright. The boat turned sharply to starboard, the wind passed behind us, and we jibed violently.

I yelled a warning, but not in time. The boom flew across the cockpit and blindsided Angelo, who, gaining confidence, had picked the wrong moment to stand up on the starboard rail and look out to sea. The impact made a thudding sound as it caught him in the stomach and knocked him over the side. I saw the splash and glimpsed a shocked expression on his face.

"Man overboard!" I yelled, and shoved Danny and Thaddeus out of the way. I took control of the helm and looked at Danny, whose mouth was open in surprise. "Go get him!" I yelled, knowing that he was a good swimmer.

After hesitating a moment, he dove over the side. "Thaddeus, don't let them out of your sight!" Humbled by his error, he nodded and watched our friends in the ocean.

I maneuvered the boat into a quick figure eight. Before I came about, Thaddeus reported that Danny had reached Angelo. I spotted them and angled to bring them alongside, dropping wind by letting the sail out as we approached. "Thaddeus, I can't leave the helm, so you're going to have to help them up. Toss Danny that line, and get Angelo on board first."

"I'm all over it, Jax."

Angelo looked pale. I stood as far to the starboard side as I could and used the tiller extension, while Thaddeus leaned down and hauled Angelo, dripping, over the port side. Their combined weight over the side tipped *Morning Sun* over pretty far.

"Good, help Angelo over to this side of the boat, then help Danny." He followed instructions. The boat tipped even farther with Thaddeus and Danny over the side, but Danny was moving faster and we were soon stable.

Everyone was breathing hard, like we'd just finished a tough game. Thaddeus and Danny looked after Angelo while I sailed back toward the marina. They said he was okay, to my relief. Angelo raised his shirt and revealed a red stripe across his upper stomach where the boom whacked him. "Got the wind knocked out of me," he said. "Felt like I got hit with a baseball bat."

"I'm just glad it didn't crack you in the head," I said.

"My fault," Thaddeus said humbly. "I was screwing around. Sorry, guys."

"Me, too," Danny said. "I knocked Fly off balance, is what happened."

Fly looked at him and smirked. "You couldn't knock me off balance with a sledgehammer," he said. "It was all my fault!"

"No, it wasn't!" Danny shouted back. "I'm the one to blame!'

"Guys, why don't you wait until we get back on land and then beat the crap out of each other," I said harshly. "You're both assholes in this situation and I don't want any more problems, so settle down!"

They both apologized to me. They had the cockiness that goes with being excellent athletes, and they rarely apologized for anything, so I knew they meant it. I was still pissed, though, and just nodded.

"Your boat, Jax," Danny added. "I should have been more respectful…hell, it's your home, too."

I wasn't in the mood to sail anymore, and from their looks, they might never set foot on a boat again. While Angelo rested below, they humbly handled the minor tasks I asked of them, and helped me clean up when we got back to my slip at the marina.

The mood lightened after we all swam at the beach and then returned to the boat for lunch. Danny cleared his throat and proposed a toast. "Here's to Thaddeus," he said, "who managed to knock his former teammate overboard less than five minutes after taking charge of the boat."

We all cheered and drank. "And here's to the old days," I said, "when they would have hanged Danny from a yard-arm for disobeying a direct order at sea."

"And here's to Jackson," he retorted, "who sails as slowly as he drives."

Angelo had the last toast. "Here's to all you jerks who talked me into this stupid trip," he said. "But thanks for saving my life. Jax, we weren't paying attention like we should have during your safety talk, but I'm really glad you insisted we wear life vests."

"Right on," Danny said. "To life vests!"

"Yeah, it was the vest that saved you, not Danny jumping in," Thaddeus said.

"Okay, okay, Danny helped a little," Angelo said.

"A little?" Danny asked. "How's that for gratitude? I should have left your little ass to the sharks."

We laughed some more, and then Thaddeus looked at me hard. "So Jax," he said, "what's happening with those goals you set?"

"Well, they changed," I said. "I've decided to join the Navy or Coast Guard for the next few years, then maybe go to a nautical college after that."

They stared at me in silence for a few moments. Then they looked at each other, back at me. Shrugs and smiles.

"That's not what I was expecting to hear," Thaddeus admitted.

"Me, either," Angelo said.

"Makes sense, though," Danny said, looking around the marina. "Being on the water seems to suit you."

"I might still play ball, in the military and later in college," I said. I planned to tell them more about it, but the words got caught in my throat. Truth was, I didn't know if I'd play basketball again. So I mumbled something about having to use the head and went below as fast as I could, before they saw the tears.

SIXTEEN

"The speed was power, and the speed was joy,
and the speed was pure beauty."

—Richard Bach

Later that day, after dinner, I thought about Danny saying I drove slowly. Kelly told me the same thing a few times, too. I knew it was my mind playing games with me, the ol' ego that Gerry talked about, but it sort of bothered me, and I decided to take out the Intruder and see what she could do.

I headed over to Route 35 and drove south past Bay Head, Ocean Beach, and Seaside Heights. After that the highway ends and the road continues into Island Beach State Park. Heavy clouds had moved in during the afternoon, so there was hardly any traffic in the park. The perfect place to rev up the bike.

After a few miles I turned back north, and in the gloomy twilight I gave her the gas. Seventy felt pretty fast on the bike, and I kept pushing, past seventy-five, past eighty. I was focused on keeping the bike straight as an arrow, but the speed finally scared me and I backed off the throttle. Glancing down, I saw the needle descend past eighty-five, so I might have hit ninety, which was fast enough for me. I was still going well over seventy when I saw the flashing lights in my mirror.

I don't know why I gunned the engine, I really don't. All I can say is that it was an instinctive reaction. The cop was far behind me and I suppose I thought I could get away. I knew I should have slowed down and faced the music, but for some reason I felt like running.

Though I gunned it past eighty, I could hear the cop gaining on me. I knew police cars were made for high speeds, and I'd heard through Angelo, whose older brother was a cop, that most of them were skillful drivers. "They like to chase people," he said. "They don't like to admit it, but my brother said it's sometimes the only fun they have all day." He'd also mentioned that hardly anyone got away, and I began to realize that my own prospects of escape were pretty bleak.

I was approaching South Seaside Park when I spotted the big hotel on the beach. I figured the cop was calling for help, and would be joined by buddies coming from town, so I pulled into the road leading to the motel. I was hoping to find a spot to hide myself and the bike among the scrub brush bordering the beach.

Then I had a better idea. The hotel was huge and had one of those fancy external elevators. The cops were probably assuming I was heading to the beach, and I was hidden from view by the brush. So I gulped a deep breath and pulled into the hotel driveway, continued under the canopy at the entrance, and went straight to the elevator. I pressed the button frantically and, as luck would have it, the door opened right away with a "ding."

I rolled inside before anyone saw me and hit the button for the second floor. The door shut and the elevator droned slowly upward. I turned the bike around, struggling with her in the small space. My heart was racing and I knew I was in a lot of trouble now...Speeding, eluding police, driving an Intruder in a hotel—they could throw the book at me.

I was thinking about the cops and didn't look before I started rolling the bike into the hallway. I nearly ran over a guy standing there. He was holding a beer and a cigarette, and looked stunned.

"Sorry," I said, turning my front wheel to go around him and half-expecting him to yell like a maniac. He recovered from his shock and stepped aside with a smile.

"No sweat, buddy," he said. Then he called back over his shoulder, "Hey Rollie, there's a dude here with a motorcycle on the elevator!"

I didn't want him to advertise the fact, of course, but his tone gave me a little hope. I shut down the engine, leaned the bike against the wall, and took off my helmet. The hallway was actually an open-air walkway with a four-foot high wall and guard rail on the outside that hid my bike from view to anyone in the parking lot.

Rollie came out of a nearby room. He was shirtless and burly, as big as Marvin Renker but softer, with hair sprouting from every pore. A crooked nose emerged from under a single brow. I wanted to be very friendly to Rollie because he looked like he would enjoy tossing people for distance.

"How you guys doing?" I offered.

They looked over my bike, then me. "Motorcycle on an elevator," Rollie said in a deep voice full of gravel. Then he smiled and stuck out his hand. "That's cool. I'm Rollie, that there's Deck."

"Like a deck of cards," Deck said.

"Hi, I'm Jackson," I said, shaking hands and feeling better. The cop siren was very loud now and we watched as he raced past the hotel driveway, heading toward the beach. I could hear more sirens, and two more cruisers turned onto the street a minute later. One continued to the beach, and one pulled into the hotel parking lot.

"Friends a yours?" Deck winked, seeing my concerned expression.

I wondered how much to trust them. What the hell, I

didn't have much to lose at this point. "I was seeing how fast the bike could go, and that first cop came after me."

"So how fast did she do?" Rollie asked.

"I backed off at around ninety." They snorted and looked unimpressed. Maybe I was destined to be a high jumper and a slow driver.

"Well," Rollie said, "guess that explains why you had a motorcycle on the elevator."

"That's it exactly."

"Want a beer?" Deck asked. I told him sure and he went to get it. The cop, meanwhile, stopped his car under the lobby canopy and went inside. He returned a minute later, and began driving slowly around the parking lot. I wondered if the clerk at the front desk saw me go by.

Deck handed me a bottle and I thanked him. "Wonder if they'll figure it out," he said.

"Ten to one against," Rollie said. "Cops ain't so smart."

"Smart enough to send your ass to prison for three years," Deck said.

"Yeah, yeah. Why you always have to bring that up?"

The other two police cars returned from the beach and rolled up next to the third in the parking lot, almost directly below where we were standing with our beers on the railing. We could hear them talking through their windows, though not well enough to make out the words. One looked up and saw us. Rollie smiled and waved and called them terrible names under his breath.

One cop exited his vehicle. "You see a guy on a motor-cycle around here?"

"No sir, Officer," Rollie said, sounding like a solid citizen. "We ain't seen no motorcycle."

"If they head up here," Deck whispered, "roll the bike into my room." I nodded, thinking I might as well add concealing evidence to my list of crimes.

The cop returned to his car. They drove out of the parking lot, two cars turning back toward town and the third going for another look around the beach. I took a sip of beer and laughed. The relief I felt was like a cool gust on a sweltering day.

"You know, Jackson, might be a good idea for you to get a room here," Rollie said. "They gonna be looking for you tonight, brother."

"Yeah, you're right," I agreed.

"Give me some cash and I'll get you a room," Deck said. "You go down, they might wonder where you suddenly appeared from with no vehicle, and call the cops back. They know us and I'll tell them we have a buddy coming in late."

I gave him the cash and he returned a short time later with the key to a room just down the walkway. I rolled the Intruder inside, shared a couple more beers and stories with my new friends, and watched a movie on cable. Then I went to sleep on land for the first time in almost three months.

SEVENTEEN

*"The sea has never been friendly to man.
At most it has been the accomplice of human
restlessness."*

—Joseph Conrad

A few days later, I walked into the boatyard in the morning and found Conrad looking over *Journey's End*, a thirty-two-foot Contessa sloop. I'd finished cleaning the interior and painting her bottom the week before.

"Nice work," he said. "The owner moved and wants her delivered down to Strathmere, south of Atlantic City. Two-day cruise. I'm closing up the Den, taking her down with you. Need to show you a few more things."

"All right," I said, excited about the voyage. "When do we leave?"

"This morning, O'Connell. Go back to *Morning Sun* and get what you need for two days. We'll be taking a limo back here after, a perk I had him throw into the deal."

At my boat, I threw some clothes and my rain gear into my backpack, along with a book and my toothbrush. The Travelift was rolling up to the boatyard when I returned. I helped get *Journey's End* off the stands and onto the hoist straps. Then Conrad handed me a hundred-dollar bill and his truck keys and told me to go over to town and buy provisions.

"I'll get her into the water," he said. "Make sure you buy enough food for five meals, just to be on the safe side. I already got some beer, but I like steak when I'm at sea. Get some instant coffee, too. Container of propane. Other than that I'll leave it up to you."

"Okay, I'll be back in an hour or so," I said. I drove off to the grocery store, making a mental list of food to buy along the way.

When I returned, Conrad sifted through the grocery bags, grunting. With Conrad, grunting was good. We cast off and he had me store the provisions below while he motored us out to the Atlantic. *Journey's End* was only eight feet longer than *Morning Sun*, but that eight feet— plus corresponding height and width increases—made an impressive difference. I could stand up and move around without feeling cramped, and actually fit in the head comfortably. I had fifty-five hundred saved so far, and I decided that when I had enough I'd buy an old sailboat, at least thirty feet long, and fix her up.

We were beyond the breakers and headed southeast when I came up to the cockpit. The day was clear and the wind was barely blowing. I put on some sun block, my hat, and sunglasses, and Conrad gave me the helm.

"Keep this heading until we're a half mile or so off the coast, then take us due south. You can put up the sails if the wind picks up to ten knots, otherwise keep motoring. We're going to duck into Barnegat Inlet and take the Intracoastal the rest of the way, just for some added security. I'm going to catch a nap. Don't wake me unless we hit a whale or lose the mast."

I told him not to worry and he went below. The drone of the inboard motor reminded me of one reason I liked sailing a sailboat so much—the relative silence. My motorcycle episode convinced me that speed wasn't for me, on land or sea. Aboard *Morning Sun* and other boats, I was content to cruise along as fast as the wind would take me, which was typically between a fast walk and running pace.

The motor was moving us down the beach, past Bay Head, Mantoloking, Normandy Beach, and Seaside Heights. After an hour the beach houses and hotels disappeared entirely and I knew we were off Island Beach State Park. In the distance I could make out the distinctive crimson top of Barnegat Lighthouse.

Yawning, Conrad stepped back into the cockpit as we neared the point. "You know where we are?" he asked.

"Yeah, Barnegat Inlet is coming up."

"Did you check the charts?"

"Sure did. We have to head northwest to get into the waterway. The tide is an hour past the slack low."

"Good," he nodded. "Why don't you take a break, make us some lunch."

He took the wheel and I went below and made us turkey sandwiches on rye. We were at the entrance to the inlet when we finished eating.

"Tricky bit of water," he said. "The long islands to the north and south force the tide through here, like a funnel. Creates a helluva current. Nothing like Deception Pass over in Puget Sound—I went through that whitewater once after I was discharged from the Navy on Whidbey Island—but strong just the same."

I nodded, having read about currents and the dangers they posed. "Sort of like a rip tide, I guess."

Conrad shot me a quick and angry look. His face turned red and his mouth vanished into his beard. "Nothing like it," he snapped. "Don't you be talking to me about rip tides. Take the damn wheel."

He stormed down below, and I wondered what I said that provoked such a reaction.

The current gave *Journey's End* a powerful push through the inlet. Our timing was good—motoring against that current, when the tide was receding, would have been a slow, fuel-consuming process. As it was, the boat was flying and I was enjoying myself.

Conrad emerged after another hour. I had us heading south in the quiet Intracoastal waters, with the mainland to starboard and Long Beach to port. We'd just passed under the Route 72 bridge.

"Any problems?"

"No," I said. "A little wind came up, but I decided to keep on motoring."

"Good decision. Let's get some miles behind us before we think about sailing. Why don't you take a break, get yourself a nap, read, whatever."

"Sure." If he wasn't going to explain why he was mad before, I wasn't going to ask. No sense risking a second eruption of Mt. Conrad. I went below and pulled out a book I'd started recently called *Dove*, about a high school dropout named Robin Lee Graham who sailed around the world by himself in the late sixties. It was an inspiring story. At times I thought I'd like to try to repeat his journey, and at times it sounded just too lonely and frightening.

The sun was dropping toward the land when I went up on deck again. Conrad was smoking a cigar and sitting in the cockpit, one finger on the wheel. "We're off Mystic Islands," he said. Pointing to the southeast he added, "That's Little Egg Inlet."

I remembered seeing it on the charts. "Where are we going to drop anchor?" I asked.

"Well, I seem to recall a protected cove on that island

dead ahead, should work fine." I checked the charts and found it—Homer's Island. The island had several coves that looked inviting.

Conrad relinquished the wheel and I followed his directions to the cove on the south side of the island. I slowed the engine and he told me what the depth sounder was reading every few seconds as we approached land. At sixty feet I let the engine idle and we drifted until the sounder read thirty feet. Conrad went to the bow and dropped the anchor, and I backed us up slowly until it gripped. He tossed out the rest of the anchor chain; we had plenty of room to revolve with the tide and current.

"Beer time," he said, and after I shut down the engine I went below to fetch us a couple. We relaxed in the cockpit and watched the sun turn from white to yellow-orange.

"Ah, that was a good day on the water," he said. "This is the first overnight cruise I've taken in ten years."

He finished his beer before I was halfway done with mine and went below to get another. I liked drinking beer with friends, but I was always aware that my father had started off the same way, and at some point the beer—and other drinks he'd developed a taste for—took control of his life. I vowed that it wouldn't happen to me, and as a result I watched how much I had and only drank in a social setting. I wanted to be able to quit any time with no problem.

Finishing up his second beer, Conrad went over and turned on the propane grill on the stern rail. I made two trips below and returned with steaks, potato salad, plates, napkins, and ketchup—and a third beer for him when he asked. We ate as the sun set and the quiet cove turned a dark blue. I'd already fallen for sailing, and now I was hooked on the cruising life.

After dinner we sat in silence and watched the stars come out. To the southwest we could make out the glow from Atlantic City. Conrad didn't seem to be enjoying the serenity of the evening, though; he sighed and grumbled to himself, oblivious that I was a few feet away, and he kept putting away the beers. I'd seen him drink before, but I'd never seen him drunk. Soon he was slurring his words and holding onto various parts of the boat for balance when he returned from the head.

"Don't say a…a damn ting…thing," he told me when I steadied him as he tilted off-balance. "Drink if…if I want to. My boat. My bo-boat."

I didn't think it was a good time to point out that it actually wasn't his boat, we were delivering it. I kept an eye on him but didn't say anything. The last thing I wanted was another physical confrontation like we'd had the first time we took the *Sunfish* out.

He looked over at me after awhile. "Your f-fault," he slurred. "Your damn fault, O'Connell."

That annoyed me. "Hey Conrad," I said, "you can get drunk if you want, but don't blame me."

"I-I'll blame you!" he yelled, leaning his head forward. His eyes were bulging with anger for a few seconds, and then suddenly turned red with tears. "Rip tide! You talk about a rip tide, you, you don-don't know what the hell you're talking about!"

"Fine, you know? I didn't mean anything by it."

"'Didn't mean anything by it,'" he mocked, wiping violently at the tears spilling down his cheeks. Leaning forward again, he yelled, "A rip tide killed my son! My wife! And you, you blather-blathering about rip tides!"

After a moment I said, "I'm sorry, Conrad. Really sorry."

He angrily waved away my apology. He reclined his head against the exterior of the cabin, under the barometer, and a few minutes later his beer bottle slipped from his hand and spilled in the cockpit. I went over and pulled him up, firmly but gently. He leaned heavily on me, barely conscious.

The steps down to the cabin were a challenge, although we managed, and I got him into the stern bunk. He sprawled and began snoring almost immediately. I watched for a few seconds and said a prayer for him. If he'd been awake, he would have interpreted the compassion I felt for him as pity, and probably cussed me out.

In the morning, I was up before dawn. I swam over to the island and ran barefoot to the Atlantic side in time to see the sun rise out of the ocean. I sprinted along the beach into the pure beauty of the new day, feeling intensely alive in the wake of the deaths that haunted my sleep.

Back on *Journey's End*, I cleaned up the cabin and the beer in the cockpit, then made myself some breakfast. I read *Dove* for an hour, then went to check on Conrad.

Still snoring away. He might not wake until noon, the way he'd been drinking, so I decided to let him sleep while I took us south.

A steady wind was blowing at nine knots off the ocean—enough to sail, fortunately, because I didn't want to wake Conrad by starting the motor. The problem is that it's hard to loosen the anchor from the bottom without motoring forward.

Then I thought of another way. I dove off the bow and followed the chain down to the anchor. The tide was low so I didn't have to go too deep. I struggled with the anchor for a few moments, then yanked it free and kicked for the surface and wonderful air.

Once the anchor was stowed, I raised the sails and took us out of the cove. I ran west with the wind between small islands until I was back in the Intracoastal Waterway, and then I turned her south. The pace was leisurely, and we didn't pass under the bridges to Atlantic City until late morning. I heard Conrad rustling down below. Talking to him would be awkward, I knew, and I was sort of dreading it. How many times can you tell a person you're sorry for what he'd been through? Apologies are boring, but I couldn't think of anything else to say.

He opened the hatch and came on deck with a cup of coffee in his hand, which I noticed was shaking a bit. He was moving slowly, squinting and generally looking like hell warmed over.

"Morning," he said.

"Morning. We have a little wind so I thought I'd sail."

"Yeah, fine." He looked around and saw the bridges behind us. "Atlantic City, the sucker's paradise," he commented.

"So you don't want to stop and play a little blackjack?" I asked.

"I'll pass," he said. He put his head down for a second, then sighed and looked up at me. "Sorry about last night, O'Connell."

"It's okay." I shrugged. "Sorry about the rip tide comment."

"No, no, not your fault. You didn't know. And that wasn't what set me off. It's the damn cruise. I haven't been on a cruise since my wife and son passed, and it brought back memories. Rip tide was just a little kindling on the fire."

"How did you deliver boats down the shore before this?" I asked.

"Trailered the small boats, subcontracted sailors I knew around the marina for the larger ones. Didn't have the heart to head out myself, 'cause of the memories. Thought I might be ready to give it another try…"

"Well, maybe you are."

"I don't know…drunken, crying fool last night." He shook his head in shame.

"Maybe you needed to do that, you know, to get it out of your system," I said, then regretted my choice of words. "I don't mean get your wife and son out of your system, I mean…"

"I know, O'Connell, I know," he said. "Could be you're right. Suppose we'll have to wait and see."

After finishing his coffee, he went to make some lunch for us. We ate in silence. He offered to take the helm afterward to give me a break, and I went below for a short nap.

The wind picked up to twelve knots and Conrad had *Journey's End* sailing along in style. We were off Ocean City, I saw on the charts. He let me take the helm and made himself comfortable in the cockpit.

"My wife's name was Angelique," he began. "I married late, and she was younger. Lovely island girl who set her sights on me for some reason. I ran a sailing charter in the Caribbean, and it was a beach party where we met. Her smile about knocked me over. I looked around, O'Connell, to see if she was smiling at someone behind me…but she wasn't."

He smiled thinking about it.

"We got married after only a few weeks, and our son was born later in the year. Named him Conrad, after me, but we called him Conner. We had a fine life. Ran the cruising charter in the islands from October to May, came up here and ran the shop in the summer, first at Atlantic Highlands and then Manasquan."

He looked down for a few minutes, then began the story again. "My son was eight when he died. We'd finished a charter with some nice folks and dropped them back in Lauderdale. It was our last charter of the season, so we decided to head out for a few days in the Bahamas before cruising north. I found a quiet cove off a little island and anchored. In the morning they wanted to swim, but the cove was rocky. There was a wide sandy beach less than a mile to the south, so they took the dinghy over."

His bright eyes seemed to dim with the sad memory. "I always thought I should have gone with them. Swimming's never been my idea of fun, and they'd gone hundreds of times alone, but I don't know...I should have kept an eye on them...They got caught in a nasty rip, pulled them out. Angelique was a born swimmer and knew about currents. She knew you swim parallel to the shore until the rip released you, or let it carry you out past the breakers until it loses energy. But Conner...he was young and didn't know. He panicked."

He took a deep breath before continuing.

"A witness on the beach said she was trying to save him, but he was struggling. They were way out, taking a beating from the waves, and they both got tired and went under. They were dead a half-hour by the time I got worried and headed over to the beach to look for them."

I told him I was sorry again. He nodded with a distant look and went below without another word. I watched the water and kept us on course for Strathmere.

EIGHTEEN

"Anchors aweigh, my boys, Anchors aweigh!
Farewell to college joys,
we sail at break of day."

—Alfred Hart Miles

When *Journey's End* was an hour from Strathmere, Conrad called the owner on his cell phone and told him to meet us at the marina. He told him to be sure to have the payment with him.

"Seems a little rude to ask for money like that," he said after ending the call. "But not everyone is trustworthy. When you're making a delivery, don't leave the boat until you have the money in your hand."

The owner was a guy named Bill McGinnis, and he and his wife Candice were very friendly. The four of us sat around the cockpit and ate the steaks Conrad cooked on the grill, and we talked about how *Journey's End* handled. Seemed a little strange to talk pleasantly about the voyage after what we'd been through. I imagined myself saying, "I found, Bill, that even if someone hurls on the deck it cleans up pretty well!" and had to stifle a laugh.

The limo arrived at eight and we settled in for the ride home. Conrad had a short nap, then told the driver to stop at a coffee stand.

"You look like you want to ask me something," he said when we were heading north on the Garden State Parkway. "Go ahead, Jackson."

"Well, I was wondering why you kept working around the ocean and boats and everything after...what happened."

"Because I love sailing and the sea," he shrugged. "I did give up long cruises, the charter business. And I haven't been back to the Caribbean in the ten years since I lost my family. But I couldn't move inland and just start over as someone else. I suppose I've been hibernating in a way, but I'm not dead. I love sailing and the sea, and you don't stop loving things because they hurt you. That's part of life."

. . .

The next week I helped Kelly move down to Princeton. She needed a small U-Haul trailer for all her things. "If you can't fit everything you own in your car," I said as I lugged another load to the trailer, "then you have too much stuff."

"Not everyone can live out of a car," she said. "Or a boat, for that matter."

Princeton was about an hour away. On the way, the guilt I was feeling about dating Lisa behind her back became too much to bear, and I told her, casually as possible, that I'd gone out a couple of times with a girlfriend of Shannon's. She pulled over at the next rest stop and parked.

"Did you sleep with her?" she asked, getting right down to it.

"No!" I said, a little outraged, although the truth was I thought about it.

"Did you kiss her?"

"Well, yeah."

"I don't believe this!" she yelled. "I go away for a week with my family and you decide to cheat on me!"

"Wait a minute, you're the one who has been putting the brakes on the relationship all summer, talking about being friends," I said.

"I also told you I loved you!"

"Some days. Other days you want to be friends and seem to regret ever using the 'L' word."

"I need to walk," she said, getting out and striding quickly away from me. She was calmer when she returned.

"I'm hurt, Jackson," she said. "I know it's not logical. You're right, I've been pushing you away, and so what you did is understandable. I still feel hurt."

"I didn't mean to hurt you, Kelly."

"Let's go," she said. "I don't want to talk about this anymore."

There really was ivy on the old walls, I noticed. The campus probably hadn't changed that much in a hundred years. Her mood improved somewhat, and she told me about some of the great minds who had walked these very lanes.

"Some good minds have walked around Glassboro State, too," I said.

"Perhaps so," she said, throwing her nose skyward, "but they simply aren't Ivy League."

"A snob, you're turning into a snob."

"Never," she protested, "although I do like the way they dress."

After getting her room arranged, we walked around the clipped lawns of the commons, played a game of chess on a bench—Kelly won but I made her sweat—and stopped at the bookstore. She pulled me away from one of the few sailing books I'd found shortly before noon. She'd mentioned that we were meeting a couple of fellow freshmen-to-be for lunch at a café near campus.

"We met when we visited in May for orientation," she explained, "and we've been e-mail pals ever since."

Her new friends were William and Ceryn—"with a C-E-Y not K-A-E," she said as we shook hands. William raised his hands as if offended by mine.

"I don't shake hands," he explained. "Nor does Donald Trump, by the way, except on TV. Given how many germs spread by hand contact, you'd think we'd have done away with that deplorable custom decades ago. The slight bow is so much more becoming."

I hated them both immediately.

While they chatted with Kelly, I looked over the menu and wondered if they let William into Princeton simply for the size of his head. It was wide and thick and seemed much too heavy for his thin neck and shoulders. A thin buzz of blond hair drew attention to his massive skull—it was hard not to stare in awe, like you were looking at Mt. Rushmore or something.

Ceryn wore a long braid and black-rimmed glasses. She liked to look at you over the top of them, as if she were grilling you before Congress and didn't believe anything you said. They seemed to like Kelly very much and despise me on sight, which I guess made us even.

On the way to the café, Kelly had casually mentioned that Ceryn was a big basketball fan and William was also a sailor. She was reaching for common denominators where none really existed, and I was surprised that she was nervous. Kelly usually didn't do nervous.

A waitress came over and smiled. I ordered a chicken sandwich on rye, and received a nasty glance from Ceryn. She made a point of ordering a salad with oil and vinegar and telling the waitress to keep out the bacon bits.

"I don't use the flesh or byproducts of animals," Ceryn explained. "I'm vegan."

William laughed. "Really, Ceryn, you don't have to

make it sound so religious. If we want to eat animals, that's our choice. It's still a free country."

"Don't you miss eating some animals?" I asked her. "Fish? Chicken? I guess I can see not wanting to eat the larger mammals because they seem almost human, but fish and chickens, well, they don't have anything better to do, right?"

"You don't have to be so crude about your disgusting habit," Ceryn fumed.

"Ceryn, you're treating us like we're smokers," Kelly said lightly. "Can you get second-hand poultry from where you're sitting?"

That amused everyone but Ceryn. "Bravo," William said. Then he informed us that Joseph Campbell argued convincingly that life consumes life, and you can't escape that fact by saying you're a vegetarian. "Campbell said being a vegetarian means that you're picking on a life form that can't run away," he concluded with a smirk.

"And you agree with that?" Ceryn asked.

"Not definitively, although he makes a valid point. I simply believe animals are a lower form of life and don't merit the same ethical consideration as humans," William said with a shrug. He looked at Kelly for approval, and I could tell he had the hots for her.

"You have to draw a moral line somewhere," Ceryn said, "and the logical place is between animals and vegetables."

"What about bugs?" I asked. "Because sometimes, you

know, bugs hang around vegetables. You might eat a few with a salad and not know it." At this point Kelly kicked me under the table and gave me a disapproving stare. I decided to shut up. Ceryn made it easy on me by switching to professors and classes and other Princeton topics. The lunch might have been okay, if not nice, but William began to feel frisky.

"So Jackson," he said shortly after our food arrived, "I hear you do a bit of sailing?"

"Yeah, I just started this summer, so I'm still learning," I said humbly, although I was actually feeling pretty competent by then.

"Ah, a novice. I've been sailing since I was seven myself. Never too late to learn something new, though. Good for you."

"Thanks," I nodded. Somehow I just knew that William wore one of those yachting caps that Conrad referred to as "sissy hats." I was equally certain that he'd never cleaned a boat in his life, and spent more time at the yacht club than he did on the water.

"Who do you sail with?" he asked.

"By myself or with friends," I said. "Sometimes with my boss at the boatyard where I work."

William looked down and smiled into his napkin, and sneaked a sideways glance at Ceryn. She chuckled and said, "He meant what club are you with?"

"Club? I'm not in a club."

"So I gathered," William said. "Not a big deal, not

really, although I must say a yacht club is the way to go if you want to meet fellow yachtsmen, take part in events, race, socialize, that sort of thing."

"I'm not interested in that sort of thing." Kelly put a hand on my arm and laughed lightly.

"Jackson's more independent," she said. "But he's an excellent sailor. He took a large boat down the coast last week."

"Wasn't that large," I said, "and I had help."

"Good thinking," William said. "Best to have a mentor in the early going. You should really get more experience before taking your friends out, though."

"Yes, I imagine it's considered bad form to return to the port with a guest or two missing," Ceryn said.

"Bad form indeed," William added. "We'd be especially concerned if you had Kelly out sailing before you were properly trained."

"He's trained just fine," Kelly said. "He's very safety conscious."

"Well that's reassuring," Ceryn said. "We want you two practicing safe boating and safe sex." She and William laughed together.

Although she was defending me, Kelly annoyed me by serving me up as a side dish to this pompous yachtsman and carnivorous vegetarian. I know she didn't mean for it to turn out this way; she probably thought she was expanding my horizons a little. Still, at this point, I thought she should be telling them off and walking out with me.

Instead, she was acting like a referee, trying to keep the fight fair.

"So how safe are you and your boyfriend?" Kelly asked Ceryn.

"I'm currently unattached," Ceryn said.

"What a shock," I said.

She ignored me and added, "I kissed Robert good-bye and wished him luck at Villanova. You have to leave your high school baggage behind when you begin college, especially at Princeton." She looked at me and put special emphasis on the word "baggage."

"Couldn't agree more," William nodded. "You need to make a fresh start, dump the ol' bilge water, as sailors say."

Baggage and bilge water, that was me. For some reason I thought all the Putdown Predators would be out of my life after high school. The one good thing about lunch with William and Ceryn was that it made me realize the predators were everywhere and I'd always have to deal with them.

While I didn't want to embarrass Kelly, I'd had enough of her new friends.

"Got to get going," I said, standing and placing some money on the table. "Hope you all have a good year."

"What?" Kelly asked, looking startled. "Where are you going? I drove, remember? And I wanted to show you around some more."

"What exactly were you going to show him, Kelly?" Ceryn asked with a lewd wink. "How spacious your dorm bed is? I can't believe you didn't get an apartment off campus. But if you've shared quarters on his little boat, maybe you'll find a way to manage."

William chuckled and added, "Pleasure to meet you, Jackson. You have a safe trip back to the boatyard. We'll have to go sailing sometime when you've learned how."

They laughed some more, pleased with their wit. Kelly was still looking shocked, and was speechless for the first time since I'd known her. She stayed in her seat.

I knew I should have just walked away and ignored them—removed my ego from the equation, as Gerry put it. But I was pissed. So I rolled up my cloth napkin and tossed it in Ceryn's face, which immediately stopped her laughter. Then, when William started to rise to confront me, I shoved him back into his seat by the shoulders, hard.

"Don't get up," I said with a warning look. I released his shoulders and he wisely stayed put. I was angry enough to punch his lights out at that point, and he knew it.

Ceryn started to loudly cuss me, drawing attention from nearby tables. I walked quickly to the door, and as I left the café I heard a waiter say that security was on the way. I picked up the pace but looked back when I was safely among the crowd of students nearby, hoping to see Kelly chasing after me. She wasn't.

I walked around having sad thoughts for a while. In downtown Princeton I bought a sailing magazine, and caught a bus back to the shore an hour later.

NINETEEN

*"When men come to like a sea life, they are
not fit to live on land."*

—Samuel Johnson

I spent most of the next morning taping off the wood and brass interior areas of *Turning Point*, a thirty-four foot Catalina, in preparation for painting. The work helped keep my mind off Kelly, more or less. I was still annoyed at her for not backing me up in front of her snotty new friends, but I wasn't actually angry, like before.

I'd thought things over on the long bus ride back to Manasquan, and on board *Morning Sun* late at night. I'd reached some conclusions about us. I wanted to cruise my thoughts some more before I called her. And I would call her, no more games. I didn't want us to end with me storming out of a restaurant.

Conrad knocked on the hull at noon. "Lunchtime," he said. "Let's get some fish burgers and talk."

Waiting for our order to arrive, he asked me about *Turning Point*. "Needs some work," I said, "but she's a nice-looking boat. Why?"

"She's owned by a friend of mine down in Florida, lives on the St. Johns River near Jacksonville. He was going to fly up and sail her down himself, but he has some business to take care of, so now he wants her delivered. I told him I had a skilled rookie who was fixing her up and could sail her down and give him a first-hand report, and he said fine."

"Wow, that's great news," I said, excited by the prospect. "You're not going to come with me?"

"Can't do it," he said, shaking his head. "Like to, but I have to keep the Den rolling until almost October. He wants her early September. So you'd be on your own all the way down the coast. Can you do it?"

There was a little challenge in his eye. "Yes, sir," I said. "I can do it."

"I know you can, Jackson. You've learned most of what you need to know, and you'll learn most of the rest on the way." After a pause, he winked and added, "But she's fully insured, just in case."

. . .

After work I ran on the beach. As I was walking back toward the marina, cooling down, I saw Kelly standing outside the gate and looking toward *Morning Sun*. I was surprised to see her. She was staring intently at the boat, looking nervous.

"Kelly," I said. "Over here."

She spotted me, and gave me that shy smile that first attracted me. "Do you hate me?" she asked.

"Pretty much the opposite," I said, and kissed her.

"Pretty much?"

"I was a little torqued, but I was going to call you," I said. "No more silent treatment between us, ever. Agreed?"

"Agreed," she said, kissing me again.

"Come on, you want something to eat?"

"Yes, I'm starved."

We ate burgers in the cockpit of *Morning Sun*, and talked it all out. "I should have followed you out of there, Jackson," she said. "I was still mad about you kissing your sister's friend—and just shocked at how rude they were. I told them off when I recovered. Believe me, all Princeton people are not like William and Ceryn."

"With a C-E-Y," I reminded her, "not a K-A-E."

She laughed and slapped my leg. "See, they're snobs, I'm not even in their league."

"Ahh, you're all Ivy League," I said, teasing her. "Just make an effort to stay snob-free during your college years."

"A promise," she said. Then she stared at the sea water in the marina, nodding, the way she did when she was deep in thought. Finally she looked up at me with those huge and intelligent brown eyes. "You know, you seem okay about me going away now."

"Yeah, I'm okay with it," I agreed. "Sorry it took most of the summer for me to realize you have to follow your dreams."

"And you have to follow yours."

"Right, that was the major problem earlier," I said. "Like we talked about. I didn't have any dreams after my sports career went down the tubes. Then they were a little fuzzy. Now I can see them shaping up. I'm going to join the Navy or Coast Guard, then maybe go to a maritime college after I've put in my four years."

"Well, that'll certainly keep you around boats and the ocean. What about basketball and track? Are you giving up that dream completely?"

"I still think about playing," I admitted. "I was just daydreaming about it during my run. But the truth is, the best I could be is a decent player at a small college. I'm not quick enough to play guard at a big school, and not big enough for forward. I don't know how I deluded myself for so long…And in track, I know I'll never jump higher than I did last spring. Some guys improve in college because they learn proper technique, but I already had excellent technique. Sounds conceited, I guess, but I know I went as high as I could."

"Which was up there," she said. "I loved watching you run and jump."

"Thanks. I always felt sort of free when I was playing

hoops with the guys, dunking, or just hanging in the air over the high jump bar. I never thought I'd feel that way again, but I do when I'm sailing, and the feeling lasts longer…It's tough to explain," I said, thinking about Gerry and his spiritual experiences.

"No, I think I understand. You look free around here," she said, gesturing around the marina. Then she pointed toward the Atlantic. "And especially out there. You just seem so at home on a boat, sailing along the ocean."

"Like you said, I plan to be around both," I said. "Having my own dreams helped put things in perspective. I understood the importance of yours. Then something Conrad said on our trip really hit me between the eyes."

"What was that?"

"He said you don't stop loving something just because it hurts you. He was talking about the sea, but I think it applies well to people, too."

"I'm sorry I hurt you, Jackson," she said, snuggling close. We kissed and talked some more, and promised to stay in touch no matter what. Maybe we would get married some day, maybe not. We'd have to wait and see.

TWENTY

*"Those who live by the sea can
hardly form a single thought of which
the sea would not be part."*

—Herman Brock

Though I put as much care into reviving *Turning Point* as I did to any other boat in the yard, knowing that she was going to be my home on the sea for a couple of weeks inspired me to double- and triple-check my work. I had her back in the water by the third week in August.

Conrad gave me more days off and didn't feel compelled to work me like a dog anymore. He'd been different since we returned from Strathmere, calling me Jackson and treating me more like a friend than an employee who sometimes pissed him off.

He came over to *Morning Sun* one afternoon holding some beers by the plastic ring, drinking the one he'd torn off.

"Permission to board my boat?" he asked.

"Come on," I said, offering a hand to help him. He freed me a beer and I handed him a couple of cushions.

"I hope you've enjoyed the summer on her," he said, "because I'm taking her back tomorrow. You move aboard *Turning Point*, and get to know every inch of her before you head down to Florida."

"Okay, that's a good idea." I looked fondly around *Morning Sun*, my first home on the sea. "I'll miss this tub."

"Tell you what, I'm looking forward to living on the water again myself," he said. "I don't know why I stayed so long in that apartment above the Den. You can fix up an attic all you want, and it's still a damn attic."

"I'm going to buy a sailboat to live on, when I get out of the service."

"Service?"

"Yeah, I've decided to enlist in the Navy or Coast Guard after I'm done with this job. Maybe go to a maritime college after. They have a couple in Florida I'm going to check out when I'm down there."

"Well all right, all right," he said smiling. "Glad you have a plan for yourself, young Jackson."

"Feels good to know where I'm headed, I'll say that.

I'm going to talk it over with my father when he comes out, get his input, but the decision is made."

"Good for you," he nodded. "I've made some decisions myself. After I close up the Den for the winter, I'm going to visit some old sailing friends up in Newport who've tried to stay in touch. Stay up there a couple weeks, then winter down in the Caribbean for the first time since...well, you know since when."

I nodded. "That's a great plan, Conrad."

"I think so. Time for me to see some old friends again, both human and otherwise. This place gets a little depressing in the winter, hardly anyone around the boats."

"I was going to take off for Florida next week, if that works for you," I said.

"Sure," he said, offering a mock toast. "Good riddance."

We talked for another hour. I told him that my father's law firm transferred him, at his request, back to New York. "He has a week's vacation before he starts," I said. "I was thinking he could crew for me on the first part of the trip. He could fly back to New York from Virginia Beach, or wherever we happen to be at the time."

"Fine by me," Conrad said. "Is he a sailor?"

"No," I admitted, "but he used to go out with friends on powerboats sometimes."

"Powerboats," he said, pronouncing the word like it tasted badly. "Well, you could teach him to sail. Just make sure he knows you're in charge. That's important."

"I'll make sure he understands," I said. "And if he doesn't, I'll go by myself."

"That's the attitude. I'll drop by and say hello to him, goodbye to you before you leave."

"Yeah, I'll let you know exactly when...Uh, my father doesn't drink anymore, so I'd appreciate it if you wouldn't bring any beer around when you meet him."

He nodded. Gerry might have told him about my family situation. I didn't want to go into the bloody details, and he seemed to understand.

"That direct speech we talked about is coming along," he said. "Got your route planned yet?"

"Yup."

"Good, but remember to be flexible. Don't get so determined to reach a destination that you ignore the weather. And Jackson, I'd advise ducking inside to the sound when you reach Carolina. Hatteras, the Outer Banks—that's shipwreck city on the windward side."

"Thanks, already planned to go inside the banks."

His eyes crinkled into a smile. "You may be a sailor yet," he said.

■   ■   ■

I called Shannon a couple of days before Jack was scheduled to arrive at Newark. "Why don't you stay over on the boat for the night?" I said. "I could come over to Red Bank and pick you up, if you want."

"No, I have some friends with cars, I can get a ride out

to the marina," she said. "I'll tell Mom I'm staying over at a friend's house, and take a cab back in the morning."

"It's not a problem for me to drive you," I said.

"No, Jackson," she said. Then she let out a long breath. "Listen, I want to see him and I don't want to see him. You know? I'll be there at five if I decide to see him. That's the way it has to be."

TWENTY-ONE

"Come, my friends, 'Tis not too late to seek a
newer world... To sail beyond the sunset, and
the baths of all the western stars... To strive,
to seek, to find, and not to yield."

—Alfred Lord Tennyson

On the last Friday in August, I finished cleaning *Turning Point* a little after three in the afternoon. I walked up the ramp, shut the gate behind me, and sat on my usual bench next to the marina parking lot. I was nervous waiting for the old man to show, and took some deep breaths, which helped.

He stepped out of a cab right on time. He looked familiar, of course, but much different than the last time

I'd seen him. He'd lost at least twenty pounds. He had more gray in his hair, but his face, free from the alcoholic bloating, looked much younger.

"Jackson," he said, walking over. I stood and we shook hands. "How have you been? I missed you."

"Missed you too, Jack," I said, looking him in the eye. He set down his suitcase, put his left hand on my shoulder, and appeared choked up. Finally we walked to the marina gate. We told each other how great we looked. He mentioned that he'd taken up yoga in addition to the long daily walks he'd been taking.

"That's very California of you," I teased, and he laughed.

We walked the docks, and I introduced him to some of the live-aboards and my new world. "And this," I said, "is *Turning Point*, our home for a while."

"Oh, a beautiful boat," he said, walking the finger pier.

"Thanks, Jack. Wish I'd taken before and after pictures, you should have seen her when I started working on her."

We boarded and I set his suitcase near the main berth and gave him a tour. He wiped a hand admiringly over the teak, noted the neatly coiled lines. "Your room was never this tidy," he said.

"Yeah, that's true," I admitted. "But nothing goes to hell faster than a boat in the water, so I've had to become neat and tidy."

A little later Conrad strolled up carrying a six-pack of soda. I introduced him to my father and they shook hands.

Conrad tossed me a plastic bag he was carrying under his other arm.

"Going away present," he said, settling himself in the cockpit. "Sorry I didn't wrap it. I don't wrap."

Inside was a new set of heavy weather gear. I pulled out the red coveralls, jacket, and boots. I knew it cost several hundred dollars. "Check it out," I said, displaying the set. "This is fantastic! Thanks, Conrad."

"Got to keep your ass dry out there," he said.

We lounged around and talked about the voyage. A little before five I excused myself and went up to the parking lot again to meet Shannon. She was five minutes late, then ten, and I concluded that she wasn't going to show. I was heading back to the gate when an old junker pulled up to the curb and she stepped out. She grabbed her backpack from the backseat and thanked her friend for the lift.

We hugged, and I told her Jack was waiting for us at the boat. "How's he seem?" she asked as we walked down the ramp.

"Just fine. He's in good shape and looks younger than he did before. You'll barely recognize him."

She was obviously nervous, and I was sure he felt the same.

I heard Conrad's deep laughter—a more common sound lately—as we approached *Turning Point*. They were telling stories, and they had plenty. Shannon was cool right up until Jack said her name and held out his hands, and then she fell apart, crying as she hugged him.

"Family reunion time," Conrad said softly to me. "I'll be going. You keep in touch, Jackson. I want to hear about your travels and adventures."

"And I want to hear about yours," I said, shaking his hand. "Thanks for everything, Conrad."

"Fair winds," he said with a wave, and walked down the pier to *Morning Sun*.

Meanwhile, Jack was still hugging Shannon and telling her he was sorry, so sorry about everything. Finally she pulled back and wiped her face with her hand. I went down to the cabin and got her a soda and some tissue.

When I returned and we were settled in the spacious cockpit of *Turning Point*, I tried to lighten the mood. "Have you talked to Lisa in the last few days?" I asked Shannon.

"No, not since last week. What's up?"

"I had a couple of dates with her," I explained to Jack. "And she had the hots for me."

"Oh, brother," Shannon laughed.

"That's me. Anyway, I called her and told her I'd made some decisions about my life and wouldn't be around here for at least a few years. I told her how much I liked her, stuff like that. Trying to let her down easy, right? I expected her to, I don't know…"

"Plead with you to stay?" Jack asked with a wink.

"Shed some tears?" Shannon asked. "Tell you her heart was breaking?"

"Well…yeah, something like that. And she just said,

'Take care, I had a fun time with you. Call me if you come back through the area, maybe.'"

They both laughed. "Lisa likes you," Shannon explained. "But she knows she's hot, and knows there are a lot of cool guys around Red Bank who aren't sailing away and joining the military."

"Just my luck. I'll never understand women."

"Join the club," Jack said.

"We have to be mysterious or it wouldn't be any fun at all," Shannon explained.

"My little girl," Jack said with admiration, "now a mysterious, beautiful young woman, giving her brother and old man sound advice."

I cooked us a fish dinner on the stern rail barbecue, and we talked through the sunset and into the night. It was after eleven when we turned in. I gave Jack the large berth in the stern. I slept in the main cabin, which had a couch and table that folded into a bunk. And Shannon slept in the V-berth in the bow.

The last time we all slept under the same roof, it was a much bigger roof…and a much sadder place. This night, the boat and sea rocked us into a sleep that, so far as I could tell, did not include past dreams and nightmares.

In the morning, we all rose early and went to breakfast at Breaker's Diner next to the marina. Shannon gave Jack another hug when her cab arrived. "Look, I'm going to tell Mom I saw you and that it was good," she said. "She's going to blow up, but I can handle her explosions. I want us to stay in touch, Dad."

"So do I," he said. "I'll call you when I get back to New York. I love you, Shannon."

"Love you too."

. . .

We spent most of the morning provisioning the boat. I gave Jack a basic sailing and safety lesson, knowing he'd learn more as we traveled. Unlike my buddies, he paid attention and seemed intent on doing things right. Still, I knew the mishap with my friends was partly my fault because I didn't set clear boundaries or take charge, and I was not going to ever let that happen again.

"Jack," I began, "I'm not saying this out of lack of respect or my own ego or anything, but you have to understand that I'm the skipper. If I tell you to do something, there's a good reason and you need to do it immediately, without any discussion. We can talk about it later, but not at the time. Can you handle that?"

He smiled softly, put his hand on my shoulder, and nodded. "You're the skipper, Jackson," he said. "I'll follow your orders. It's your boat."

"'She,'" I said with a smile. "A boat is always 'she.'"

. . .

I double-checked my list and took a last look around my summer home. My father cast us off, a little harder than necessary, and he had to run along the finger pier to catch up to the boat. I went to the port rail and extended my arm. We clasped each other's forearm, and I pulled him aboard.

I motored *Turning Point* out of the marina, soaking up all the familiar sights one last time, then headed us south when we passed the jetty.

"Want to take the wheel, Dad?" I asked. "Wind's blowing almost ten knots. I'm going to raise the sails."

"Sure, be my pleasure," he said. Neither of us said anything about it, but I couldn't keep calling him Jack. It didn't sound right, and it wasn't necessary anymore.

"The tendency is to over-steer," I told him as he put his hands on the wheel; I noticed how much they looked like my hands. "It takes a while to develop a feel. Head us southeast."

"Aye-aye, Captain," he said. He said it with pride rather than irony.

While hauling up the mainsail with the halyard, I thought of the world before me and the one I was leaving behind. In my wake were my major family problems, my high school friends, my sports dreams.

Sunset and sunrise

And of course there was Kelly, our bittersweet love, our separate paths, and the possibility that they might cross again some day.

Highlights in eyes

I tied off the halyard and looked at the Jersey shore passing slowly alongside, and thought of all the great things I'd seen this summer, from lights shimmering on the water to all the beautiful sailboats.

Symbols and signs

Then I looked at the sky, the wispy white clouds that I knew would turn dark and frightening at times, testing my courage and skills.

Mystery of air

I considered the other men and women who lit out for adventure before me.

Sailing worn trails

And I watched my father at the helm, aware of the pain he'd caused, now seeking forgiveness and grace.

Above earthly wails

And finally I turned to the great ocean before the bow, and gratefully gave thanks for Granny and Gerry and Conrad, who helped me find the freedom I loved and would always prize.

To the blue beyond baseballs

THE END

John Foley is a writer and teacher in Vancouver, Washington. He lived on a sailboat for a year in the Puget Sound area, and continues to enjoy sailing, kayaking, and hiking.